PRAISE FOR THE BOOKS OF
#1 INTERNATIONAL BESTSELLING AUTHOR
KERK MURRAY

Since the Day We Wished

"I read it in one sitting! If you love small town romance with realistic characters, you need to read this. I already pre-ordered the next one."
— Reader Review

"That ending had me sobbing. Such a beautiful story about healing."
— Reader Review

"Loved every page. The Wishing Tree concept was so romantic and unique. Kerk Murray is an auto-buy author for me now."
— Reader Review

"I hope this gets made into a movie. So good!"
— Reader Review

"I want to live in Hadley Cove! Phil's Diner need to be real."
— Reader Review

"Not your typical romance. I loved how the story dealt with real life issues in a relatable way. I felt like I was there side by side experiencing everything with the characters."
— Reader Review

"Read it twice already this week. It's the perfect comfort read."
— Reader Review

"Finally, a romance that handles grief with so well!"
— Reader Review

"The writing pulled me right in. I found myself cheering for the Katie and Sam multiple times. Also, seeing some of the side characters from the previous books in the series was great!"
— Reader Review

Since the Day We Kissed

"This is the first romance I've read written by a male and won't be my last by this author. His take on romance was surprisingly insightful—you can't help but cheer for Kara and Ethan."
— Reader Review

"The best story in the series by far!"
— Reader Review

"I can't wait to read more Kerk Murray books! He's my favorite new-to-me author."
— Reader Review

"I absolutely adore Hadley Cove! It felt like I

was returning to my hometown."

— Reader Review

"The plot twists in this book caught me off guard in the best way possible. They kept me on my toes without sacrificing the emotional core of the story."

— Reader Review

"Murray nails the bittersweet nostalgia of first love. I'm pretty sure I just felt every emotion known to mankind."

— Reader Review

Since the Day We Fell

"Hadley Cove feels like a character in itself. It's a place that feels both real and magical and one that I never want to leave."

— Reader Review

"Kerk has a gift for capturing the nuances of human emotion. I found myself stopping to

highlight several passages."
— Reader Review

"I've been a fan of Kerk's work since *Pawprints On Our Hearts*, and *Since the Day We Fell* did not disappoint."
— Reader Review

Since the Day We Danced

"Murray's writing is simply gorgeous."
— The Book Commentary

"An emotional rollercoaster that will make you fall in love with love all over again."
— Reader Review

"A beautiful escapist Nicholas Sparks type romance."
— Reader Review

Pawprints On Our Hearts

"Animal lovers will feel connected to Murray's almost spiritual awakening and admire his devotion to following his heart, even in the face of tremendous sacrifice. This touching memoir overflows with intense emotion."
— Booklife by Publishers Weekly

"A deeply moving memoir... one of the best books that capture the connection between human beings and dogs... *Pawprints on Our Hearts* inspires a love for animals while exploring the painful edges of the human heart in need of love and healing."
— The Book Commentary

"A powerful and emotional story."
— Alyson Sheldrake, Bestselling author of "Kat the Dog"

Since the Day We Wished

KERK MURRAY

Since the Day We Wished

Hadley Cove Sweet Romance: Book 4

Magnolia Press
Birmingham

Copyright © 2025 by Kerk Murray

All rights reserved.

The story, all names, characters, and incidents portrayed in this production are fictitious. No identification with actual persons (living or deceased), places, buildings, and products is intended or should be inferred.

No part of this publication may be reproduced, distributed, or transmitted in any form or by any means, including photocopying, recording, or other electronic or mechanical methods, without the prior written permission of the publisher, except as permitted by U.S. copyright law. For permission requests (other than for review purposes), please contact info@kerkmurray.com.

Magnolia Press
105 Vulcan Rd
Ste 221
Birmingham, AL 35209

Library of Congress Cataloging-in-Publication Data

Names: Murray, Kerk, author.
Title: Since the Day We Wished/ Kerk Murray.
Description: First edition. | Birmingham: Magnolia Press, 2025.
Identifiers: LCCN (pending) | ISBN 9798985116199 (paperback) | ISBN 9798992553802 (hardcover)

Printed in the United States of America

To the ones who've stopped making wishes. May this story remind you to start again—this one's for you.

Before You Begin...

You're invited to join my private Facebook Reader Group, where you'll make new book friends, meet other animal lovers, and be the first to know about new releases, book clubs, and special deals.

Join today:
Kerk Murray's private Facebook Reader Group

facebook.com/groups/779562103953550

Listen on your favorite music streaming platform.

kerkmurray.com/products/sincethedaywewishedplaylist

Katie's Listens

1. "Stronger (What Doesn't Kill You)" — Kelly Clarkson

2. "Brave" — Sara Bareilles

3. "This Is Me" — Keala Settle, The Greatest Showman

4. "Begin Again" — Taylor Swift

5. "Who Says" — Selena Gomez

6. "Survivor" — Destiny's Child

7. "At Last" — Etta James

8. "Firework" — Katy Perry

9. "When You Wish Upon A Star" — Leigh Harline & Ned Washington

10. "Perfect" — Ed Sheeran

Sam's Listens

♪♫

1. "Chasing Cars" — Snow Patrol

2. "I Wish You Would" — Taylor Swift

3. "Home" — Phillip Phillips

4. "Just The Way You Are" — Bruno Mars

5. "The Sound of Silence" — Disturbed

6. "All of Me" — John Legend

7. "My Wish" — Rascal Flatts

8. "Hall of Fame" — The Script

9. "Amazed" — Lonestar

10. "I'm Yours" — Jason Mraz

Dear Reader,

I'm thrilled to welcome you back to Hadley Cove for the forth book in this series.

As I wrote this book, I found myself contemplating the nature of wishes—not just the kind we make on shooting stars or birthday candles, but the ones that live quietly in our hearts. Wishes are reflections of who we are and what we long for, even when we're afraid to admit it. Some wishes fade, while others stay with us, waiting for the right moment to come true. And some wishes will even lead us down the most unexpected paths to exactly where we were meant to be.

In this story, you'll meet Katie and Sam, two people who have lost so much yet still have so much to give. Their journey is about second chances, not just in love, but in rediscovering the courage to believe in something bigger than themselves.

I hope you feel the charm of the Breezy Tails Bookshop, hear the rustling wishes tied to the Wishing Tree, and perhaps even reflect on the wishes of your own heart. Above all, I hope you'll remember that even the most ordinary moments can hold extraordinary possibilities.

Thank you for being a part of this incredible adventure and for joining me in creating a more compassionate world for all living beings, one heartwarming story at a time.

Your support through reading and sharing this series, along with your kind words in messages and reviews, means more than I can express. I'm forever grateful.

Don't forget to check out the extras I've included at the front and end of the book, created with you in mind.

"I wish you to know that you have been the last dream of my soul."

—Charles Dickens, *A Tale of Two Cities*

1

Katie

October

Thursday

"Oh no, no, no—"

Katie lunged for the tipping stack of books, her stool wobbling beneath her. She caught the top of the pile just in time, but one book still tumbled, landing with a soft thud, spine-up on the floor.

Of course, it was *Pride and Prejudice*. Romance novels always made the most dramatic exits at the Breezy Tails Bookshop.

"At least stick to your own section," she muttered as she hopped off the stool. She scooped up the book and gave it a gentle dust-off before sliding it back into its rightful spot.

Katie squared her shoulders and turned toward the counter, raising a hand to shield her eyes from the late afternoon sun streaming through the windows.

Jingle. Jingle.

Glancing over her shoulder at the front door, Katie saw her friend enter. "Em!"

Emma grinned. "Hey, you!" The redhead bent down to pat the graying muzzle of Katie's rescue dog, an elderly miniature schnauzer, who snoozed in his usual corner. "And hello to you too, Benny boy."

Katie straightened her faded T-shirt as she moved to greet Emma, but her gaze fell on a nearby shelf with wooden slats that bowed under the weight of too many books. She bit her lip as her list of things to fix grew longer.

"Katie?"

She blinked, returning her attention to Emma. "Yes? I mean, yes, I'm here. Heh. So, what brings you by today?"

"That, that right there." Emma smirked.

"What? The shelf? I plan on fixing it, after the register, and the leak, and the—"

"That's not what I meant. *You* are what I meant, because if you don't give yourself a break, nothing is gonna get fixed. Besides, someone's gotta make sure you remember what sunlight looks like, yeah?"

Katie's laugh trailed off into a sigh. "A break?" She shook her head, combing a stray strand of hair behind her ear before reaching behind the counter. The familiar heft of her battered toolbox settled in her hand as she left the counter and crossed over to the sagging shelf. Then, crouching down, she set the toolbox beside her. Metal clinked as she fished out a hammer and a handful of bent nails. "I appreciate the thought, as always, but the to-do list won't do itself."

"But you're always fixing something around here."

"It's part of its charm," Katie chirped. The hammer's taps echoed through the shop, and Katie winced at each impact, half-expecting the shelf to collapse, or the hammer to hit her thumb.

But none of that happened—yet.

Stepping back, Katie eyed her handiwork and gave a nod before rising to her feet. She swiped at her jeans, which left pale streaks across the denim.

"You know, if you ever need an extra set of hands around here, say the word." Then, with a mischievous grin, Emma added, "Or we could always ditch the DIY for some wine and Lorelai Gilmore's latest crisis. Your call."

Katie released a small, contented sigh. She was lucky to have a friend like Emma. Someone who understood, who was always there. "Ugh, I wish. Wine night and drifting away to Stars Hollow sounds pretty great about now."

As she returned her toolbox to its usual nook, Katie's gaze swept over the shop—the worn shelves, outdated carpet, and the paint flaking from the walls. To some, it might seem run-down. But to her, it was *home* in every sense of the word—from the beloved bookshop below, to the creaky stairs leading up to her small apartment. She loved the chirping chorus of birds that greeted her each morning and the clear view of stars twinkling through her bedroom window at night. It was simple, yet it was everything.

"So," Katie said brightly, pivoting toward Emma, "what's

new with you? How's business at Barking Orders?"

"Can't complain," Emma said, rummaging in her bag and stepping closer. "Speaking of which—look what I brought for Benny!" She brandished a colorful package and set it on the table. "Ta-da! Our latest creation. Peanut butter and sweet potato flavored treats. I figured Benny might want to try something new."

"You always know how to spoil him, don't you?" Katie looked over to Benny. The old dog's chest rose and fell in a rhythm, his paws twitching slightly at some unseen dream. "Thank you, Em. Seriously."

"Ah, it's nothing," Emma said, waving her off before looking toward Benny. "How's the little guy holding up these days?"

"Oh, you know. A little arthritis and more naps than ever, but still the sweetest boy around." She chuckled. "What about your little escape artist? Riley still giving you a run for your money?"

Emma rolled her eyes dramatically. "Don't even get me started. The little terror almost gave me a coronary this morning. I swear, he sees that gate as a personal challenge."

Katie shook her head. "Some things never change, huh? Brings back memories of our first ... encounter."

Emma let out a breath, as if reliving the episode all over again. "What a day that was. I heard those brakes and my heart stopped. And then I saw your face—thought for sure you'd flattened him. Glad he only ran himself into the car though, and not the other way around."

"Right?" Katie chimed in. "I was so relieved and so very sorry, Emma. I would never—"

"Breathe …" She reached out, squeezing Katie's arm. "I got me a pretty great friend out of the deal, and Riley's doing just fine."

Katie gave a half smile. "Yes, you did, I did, he is."

"You're still not breathing."

"Oh, right—" Katie took a deep breath.

The tinkling of the bell above the door drew their attention as an elderly woman stepped inside.

Katie hurried over. "Welcome to Breezy Tails. What can I help you with today?"

The woman's face crinkled into a smile. "Oh, don't mind me. I'm just happy to see this place is still open. It's been ages since I set foot in here. More years than I'd like to count," she said, fiddling with her glasses. "But I remember coming here as a girl with my father. He always said this was the best place in town to find a good story. Although, back in the day, it was called something different, wasn't it? It was … hmm … I think it was—Oh, blast this old memory!"

"It's okay. It was a long time ago. Well, perhaps not too long. I took over this place two years ago, which I bet is hardly a blink for—" Katie caught Emma's eye from across the room as she raised a hand in a calming gesture, reminding her to breathe.

Inhale … Exhale … Turning back to the older woman, Katie began again. "Why don't you tell me a little about what you like to read, and we'll see if we can find the perfect—well, not perfect, nothing is perfect—but the best book for you."

The woman beamed. "Oh, you're so kind. Let's see, I've always loved stories with characters who make you think a little. A dash of romance is lovely, too. I once read this book that hooked me within the first few pages ..." As Katie listened, she guided the woman toward the shelf she had just repaired. "Mhm ... yes ... I see ..." She stopped at the romance section, and her nodding slowed as the customer's words faded, leaving them in a stretch of uncertain silence.

The woman cleared her throat. "So, do you have anything like that?"

Katie blinked. "Oh! Oh yes, sorry, I wasn't sure if you were done and I didn't want to interrupt. But I think I have what you're looking for."

As Katie scanned the shelf, her fingers led the way, moving along the spines before stopping decisively. Then she pulled out the book, presenting it with a flourish. "How about *Pride and Prejudice*? It's a classic for a reason."

The woman took the offered book, cradling it as she admired the crimson cover and the title's gold lettering. "Oh my, I've heard of this one, but I've never read it," she admitted. "What's it about?"

"Everything. I mean, it's got everything—romance, wit, and a heroine you'll adore. Elizabeth Bennet's a firecracker, especially when it comes to Mr. Darcy—trust me, you'll want to shake him at first, but there's more to him than meets the eye, not that I want to spoil it." Katie took another breath, and on the exhale felt the tension ease out of her shoulders. "It's about love, acceptance, and learning to see people for who they really are ..."

Katie's voice wavered, and for a split second, images of her failed marriage flashed through her mind—how she'd once thought she understood Derek, only to see everything unravel. Thankfully, she'd had Jane Austen to keep her together. Blinking, she shook off the memory and forced a smile back to her face. "It's one of those stories that stays with you."

"This sounds wonderful." The woman's enthusiasm faltered. "I hate to ask, dear, but—well, things have been tight lately. Fixed income and all. Is there any chance of a small discount? These old bones don't bring in what they used to, you see."

The store's most recent profit-and-loss statement flickered in Katie's mind, reminding her of how thin her margins had become. Even so, she lifted her chin and brushed the thought aside. Forty-three years of life had taught her that kindness usually found its way back around. "Of course," she said without hesitation. "Let's call it a special 'welcome back' discount. After all, it's not every day we get to reunite a reader with their childhood bookshop, is it?"

The old woman smiled and thanked her as Katie walked her to the counter and checked her out.

After the customer left, Emma approached the counter. "Katie, I get it, I do. This place is your baby, and you love these customers, but—"

"It's fine, Em. I can manage. I always have," Katie insisted, straightening a nearby stack of business cards. "A few dollars here and there isn't going to sink us. It'll build customer loyalty."

"Really? And when was the last time you actually paid yourself? You're pouring everything into this place"—Emma paused—"but who's looking out for you in all of this?"

She's right, but ...

Katie's hands balled into fists before she shoved them into her pockets. "I'm managing just fine," she said, her tone a little sharper than she intended. She closed her eyes and unclenched her jaw, trying to soften her voice. "I'm sorry, I didn't mean to—but look, I know it's not ideal, okay? But it's nothing I can't handle. I've got this."

Emma stepped closer. "I know you do, but I also think you deserve better. You work so hard—you can't keep putting yourself last."

Katie's chest tightened at the words. Maybe she *did* deserve better—better than this constant struggle, better than what she'd let herself believe when she'd been married to Derek.

She remembered the day Derek had found her old journal, the one where she'd written about opening her own bookshop someday. He'd laughed, not unkindly at first, but then: "You can barely keep our house in order. How would you ever manage an entire store?"

The familiar sting surfaced as Katie drew in a steady breath, willing the memory to fade.

Stay later. Work harder. Do better.

"I just need to keep things running," Katie murmured, her hands fidgeting with a stray pen on the counter.

Emma nudged Katie. "Hey, you know what? The Wishing Tree Festival is kicking off soon." Her voice brightened. "We should check it out."

Katie paused and reached for her spiral notebook by the register, flipping it open. The notebook's pages fanned beneath her thumb—a record of patches and prayers over the past two years. Some entries were crossed out. Most weren't.

When she arrived at her latest entry, her pen hovered over the page, already crowded with her cramped handwriting and five reasons to stay put:

Fix fan before it falls.

Redo window display (summer books still out)

Deep clean carpet - check rental costs?

Replace stair treads (ALL of them this time)

Find source of leak - call plumber?

She began adding estimated costs beside each task, then stopped—some numbers were better left unwritten.

"C'mon. When's the last time you did something just for fun?" Emma wiggled her eyebrows. "We could make a wish. Drink pumpkin spice lattes. Be basic fall girlies. Live a little, you know?"

Maybe she's right. It's not like these problems won't still be here in an hour. Or two.

"You know what?" Katie closed the notebook. "A pumpkin spice latte sounds perfect right now."

Emma's face lit up. "Wait. No argument? Who's this girl, and what've you done with my Katie?"

"Don't get used to it," Katie laughed, already reaching for her jacket.

After slipping it on, she grabbed Benny's leash.

Benny's ears perked up. "Hey, old man," she called softly. "What do you say we go on an adventure, huh?"

He rose from his bed with a stretch and gave a little shake before his tail set to wagging.

Katie clipped the leash to his collar and locked up the store. As they walked toward Main Street, the autumn breeze carried hints of caramel, cinnamon, and freshly baked pretzels. String lights crisscrossed overhead between lampposts, swaying in the cool afternoon air. The sound of an acoustic guitar floated above the growing crowd, mixing with children's laughter and the excited chatter of festival-goers.

As they reached the entrance, a familiar voice called out from behind. "Katie! Hold on a second, honey."

Katie turned to see Ms. Dottie, the town's longtime courier, hurrying toward her, an envelope in hand. Her gray curls peeked out from beneath her cap, and her mailbag was slung over one shoulder.

"I just missed you at the store," Ms. Dottie said, stopping in front of Katie. "This one needed a signature, and I wasn't about to leave it in your mailbox. Saw you heading this way and figured I'd catch up."

Katie took the envelope. "A signature?"

Ms. Dottie shrugged. "Not my business what's inside, just making sure it gets to the right hands. Just sign here real quick."

She handed Katie a small clipboard, and Katie signed.

"Thanks, Ms. Dottie."

"Anytime, sweetheart." Ms. Dottie tucked the clipboard back into her bag, then gave Benny a quick pat on the head. "Be good, you." She glanced at Emma with a nod. "You too, kiddo."

With a wink, she adjusted her bag and headed off.

For a second, Katie stared at the envelope, turning it over in her hands, before tearing it open. Her pulse quickened as she unfolded the letter, the words blurring momentarily before she forced herself to focus.

Dear Ms. Hayes,

This notice is to inform you that your property, Breezy Tails Bookshop, has been found to be in violation of the Hadley Cove Building Code, Section 5.2, which states that all commercial structures must be maintained in a safe and habitable condition.

Our inspection has revealed significant structural issues, including water damage, unstable shelving, and potential electrical hazards. Below is a detailed breakdown of the identified violations:

1. Water Damage: Evidence of mold growth on interior walls and near shelves, posing a health risk.

2. Unstable Shelving: Antique shelving units improperly secured, posing a risk of tipping under the weight of books.

3. Electrical Hazards: Outdated wiring in the main storage room and customer seating not compliant with current safety standards.

4. Foundation Issues: Cracks along the building's foundation, causing uneven flooring in the storage room.

5. Fire Safety Violations: Emergency exit signage not properly illuminated or visible.

6. Plumbing Issues: Poor drainage in outdoor gutters contributing to water pooling near the foundation.

7. HVAC Concerns: Blocked or dirty vents causing inadequate airflow and potential health risks.

8. Structural Integrity: Bowing in the main support beams posing a risk to the building's stability.

9. Accessibility Concerns: Uneven door thresholds limiting wheelchair access.

10. Lighting Issues: Insufficient lighting in customer areas, posing safety risks for employees and customers.

You have 21 days to bring your property up to code. Failure to do so may result in fines and/or possible condemnation of the property. If you have questions, please contact our office at 912-555-4617.

Sincerely,
Raymond Barnes
Chief Building Inspector

Katie's breath hitched, going over the words again, as if reading them a second time might make it less catastrophic. But no—*twenty-one days* was all she had. Her stomach knotted, and nausea crept up her throat, turning the ground beneath her feet unsteady.

How can I fix everything in that time? The repairs alone—a fortune I don't have. And my home, what about my ...

Her thoughts darted to the little apartment above the shop, to the only place that had ever felt truly hers, the place where she pieced herself back together after the divorce ... and now all of it was slipping away, being taken away—

Katie felt a hand press to her back.

"What is it? What's wrong?" Emma asked.

But Katie couldn't speak. Her mind spiraled, thoughts colliding and dissolving into panic.

She glanced at the inspector's name at the bottom of the letter. He had stopped by last month, smiled casually, and assured her there were only minor issues, a few small repairs here and there. Nothing urgent. And now—*this.*

Was he lying then?

Or is this all some kind of mistake?

The letter made it all sound like the entire building ... Her entire world was on the verge of collapse.

The festival buzzed around her, the once-inviting sounds now grating. Katie's eyes drifted to the Wishing Tree, its ribbons fluttering in the breeze, each one tied with someone's hopes. Tiny fairy lights threaded through the branches like sleeping stars, waiting for dusk to wake them. But wishes were for dreamers. She needed something more ...

She needed a miracle.

2
Sam

Just drive. Don't think about her. Just keep driving.

Sam Everett had whispered those words like a prayer during the four-hour drive from Greenville, South Carolina. And now, as his old pickup rattled over the familiar roads, the mantra was all that kept him from turning around and driving away again.

He rolled the windows down as he neared Hadley Cove, hoping the cool breeze might clear his head. Instead, the sea air swept in, reminding him of all he'd lost.

Elizabeth had lived for moments like this. "Sam, look," she'd say, squeezing his hand. "It's like we're living in a painting." Long shadows stretched across Hadley Cove's streets, as the afternoon sun covered the quaint cottages and local shops in the kind of golden light she had once adored.

There was an undeniable magic in how the sun could turn the old pastel buildings into something almost otherworldly. But now, to Sam, the colors—although still there, still beautiful—felt empty, like the life they once held had faded along with her.

Sam's grip on the wheel tightened as he passed the park where they had first met. He had been on his lunch break, drawings of buildings spread across the hood of his truck, trying to figure out why a twelve-foot support beam didn't align with the fifteen-foot foundation design for the Wilson project. Elizabeth had been reading under the town's Wishing Tree, which he approached to escape the summer heat, wiping sawdust from his hands onto his jeans.

He'd managed nothing more eloquent than a comment about the weather, but she had smiled and asked about his work. Before he realized it, he was rambling about blueprints and measurements, while she shared her dreams of running her grandmother's bookstore one day—but one day never came ...

Passing Morgan's Ice Cream Parlor, it was as if Elizabeth's laugh still lingered there, near the wooden bench outside, where they had spent their first date sharing a banana split. He'd been so nervous he had dropped his spoon twice, and she'd gotten ice cream on her nose. Neither had finished their half, too busy stealing glances at each other. Every July after, they'd make the drive from Greenville to share a banana split on that same bench, laughing and marveling at how lucky they were to have found each other.

Around the corner was the coffee shop where they had planned their future over strawberry croissants. Elizabeth would sketch house designs on napkins with quick, sure strokes—the window seat she had always wanted, the workshop he would need. Sam had teased her about the impractical rooftop garden she'd drawn, and she'd laughed, telling him, "We'll sort out the details tomorrow. Today's for dreaming." It was such a small thing, but it had stuck with him—the way she always left room for tomorrow, as if it would always be there.

Sam released a heavy sigh, knowing better than anyone that some days, loving someone meant carrying their memory in places only you could see. The worst part hadn't been losing her—it was learning how to begin again while keeping her story safe.

Ten years.

His hand went to his chest, pressing against his sternum as if that could ease the familiar tightness there. He muttered a curse and adjusted the rearview mirror, more to ground himself than out of necessity. "Washington, Adams, Jefferson ..." The names rolled off his tongue, just like Mrs. Henderson had drilled into their fourth-grade heads.

He exhaled slowly and forced his focus back to the road. By the time he reached Lincoln, the street had curved past the last cluster of downtown shops—Phil's Diner, Walker's Pharmacy— before revealing the ocean ahead. Further down, the sign for the Sandy Shores Inn came into view, and Sam turned into the parking lot.

The two-story inn stood against the coastline, its powder-blue exterior framed by crisp white trim. The scene looked impossibly perfect, like someone had staged the whole thing for a tourism brochure—and somehow it all felt less real because of it. Brown shingles capped the roof, weathered just enough to suggest charm rather than neglect. Sam climbed out of his truck and squinted at the wraparound porch where rocking chairs swayed beneath hanging baskets bursting with bright flowers. Wooden wind chimes jangled from above. He blinked hard as a pair of sparrows darted to the bird feeder on a nearby post.

His boots scraped against the wooden steps as he approached the entrance. Light caught the brass kickplate like a camera flash, making him hesitate before he pushed through the white storm door. He made it two steps into the lobby before a furry missile hit his legs. A chocolate Lab, tail thumping against the doorframe, looked up at him with eyes that held no judgment—just pure joy. Sam's hand found the soft spot behind the dog's ears, and briefly, he felt something in his chest loosen.

"Daisy, down girl!" A woman's voice called out from behind the front desk. "I'm so sorry about that. She just can't help herself sometimes. Total attention hog." The innkeeper's blonde hair was pulled back in a neat bun, revealing bright green eyes that sparkled with kindness. "Lisa, by the way. Welcome to the Sandy Shores Inn."

"Sam," he replied, continuing to pet Daisy. "And no need to apologize for the dog."

"Noah!" Lisa shouted toward the back of the inn. "Can you come grab Daisy? We have a guest!" She turned back to Sam and offered an apologetic smile. "My husband's out back setting up new patio furniture. I'd grab her myself, but—" She held up her freshly painted coral nails with a sheepish grin.

A man's voice carried from somewhere behind. "Coming!"

Lisa slid the registration paperwork across the desk. "While we wait, let's get you checked in. Just need you to fill these out." She grabbed a pen from the ceramic Sandy Shores mug and held it toward him. "Planning to stay with us long?"

"A week or so," Sam replied, taking the pen and beginning to fill out the paperwork.

"What brings you to town?" Lisa asked, sorting through room keys hanging on the wall behind her.

"Work." He paused, then added, "Contract work. Done a few jobs around here before. What's one more?"

A man appeared through the back door in a Sandy Shores polo, carefully taking hold of Daisy's collar. His eyes met Sam's with a friendly directness. "Welcome. I'm Noah."

"Sam. Nice to meet you," he said, sliding the completed forms back to Lisa.

Lisa took the paperwork and handed Sam a key that dangled from a seashell keychain. "You're in room 108, right down that hallway to the left. Breakfast is served from seven to ten in the sunroom, and our café is open for lunch and dinner until eight." She glanced both ways like she was about to share a secret. "Also, our peach cobbler muffins, I hear they're kind of a big deal."

"Thanks. Might have to try one," Sam said with a half-smile, taking the key and heading down the hallway with his bag.

At room 108, he jiggled the key in the stubborn lock before the door finally gave way. Then, stepping inside, he let the door fall shut behind him with a *click*.

The room was small but clean; its honey-toned hardwood floors and whitewashed walls gave it a nautical feel. In the corner, a desk paired with a mismatched chair stood like an afterthought. The bed was neatly made, covered by a faded blue-and-yellow quilt that had the uneven stitches of something handmade. A single window overlooked the parking lot, though salt-streaked blinds partially obscured the view. The faint smell of lemon cleaner hung in the air, trying its best to mask the ever-present briny scent of the ocean. Not unpleasant, but unmistakably temporary. Just like most things in his life these days.

As he arranged his belongings around the modest room, Sam found Derek Huntington's business card tucked away in one of his bags. He had done three renovation projects along the Georgia coast for Derek in the past year—small stuff, mostly updating old beach houses into vacation rentals.

But this time was different. Derek had been vague about the details, only said it would be Sam's biggest project, and handed him a check that made that clear enough. This contract, which had brought him back to Hadley Cove for the first time since Elizabeth's passing, was worth more than all his previous jobs combined.

Sam stared at Derek's business card, his thumb absently tracing its embossed letters until the edge began to curl. Despite his reservations about the project and Derek's unusual silence about the specifics, the envelope from the county hospital sitting on his kitchen table back home left little room for a conscience. Elizabeth's life insurance had barely—he shoved the card into his wallet. The why didn't matter anymore. Only the work did.

His stomach growled, reminding him he hadn't eaten since leaving Greenville. Although food was the last thing on his mind, he eventually wandered to the café, ordered a coffee and a peach cobbler muffin, and found a quiet corner table. After one bite, Lisa's words came rushing back.

"She's right," he muttered, taking another bite, then another, more out of enjoyment than hunger. The muffin was sweet, but not too sweet, with chunks of fresh peaches, and it had just the right amount of crumble.

From the next table over, conversation drifted like the steam off his coffee.

"Can you believe what that developer wants to do to this place? First the old library, now this?" A man grumbled, shaking his head.

"All in the name of 'progress,'" a woman replied with an eye roll.

"Derek Huntington—" The man's gaze followed a passing server. "He's buying up everything he can get his hands on."

Sam's grip tightened around his mug as the words *progress* and *Derek Huntington* churned in his mind.

"We've already lost so much," the woman added. "That man will be remembered as the man who destroyed what made this place special."

"Change is inevitable, I suppose. Not much we can do," the man said. "But that doesn't mean we have to like it."

Sam's coffee turned bitter in his mouth. His fingers drummed against the ceramic mug. He recalled his initial phone conversation when Derek had sold him on this project as an opportunity to grow, but the townspeople's tones suggested something else entirely.

He took a slow breath, steadying himself.

I gotta look out for me. Can't be blamed for that.

Rising to his feet, Sam brushed the crumbs from his hands, crumpled the muffin wrapper, and tossed it into the trash. He then downed the rest of his coffee in one quick gulp before adding the mug to the growing collection in the bin.

Though the long drive and the week ahead weighed on him, the thought of going back to his room felt stifling. He needed air.

The screen door clattered behind him as he stepped onto the porch, where October winds whipped off the water. His skin pebbled instantly.

Should've grabbed my jacket.

Ahead, the beach lay nearly empty, save for a few figures bundled in thick sweaters. They plodded across the sand, shoulders hunched, and heads bowed against the gusts. Sea grass swayed on top of the rolling dunes. Foam-tipped waves crashed along the shoreline, their spray turning to amber and rose in the fading light of day. Further down, a cluster of colorful beach houses perched on stilts overlooked the water.

"Beautiful, isn't it?" Lisa's voice carried over the sound of the waves as she stepped outside.

Sam turned, catching the sunset mirrored in her eyes. He gave a small nod. "Yeah. It really is."

For a moment, neither of them spoke as the waves and squawking of seagulls filled the silence.

The townspeople's concerns gnawed at his conscience once more.

Will my biggest project end up being my biggest mistake?

Maybe so. At forty-five, he should've known better than to take a job without knowing all the details. But right now, being wrong paid better than being right—and he needed the money more than he cared to admit.

Lisa's voice interrupted his thoughts. "If you're free tonight or this weekend, you might wanna check out the Wishing Tree Festival. It ends on Sunday. It's right down the road."

The Wishing Tree Festival ...

Sam's mind drifted to two years ago when Elizabeth had insisted on going, even though the treatments had left her so weak she wobbled with every step. He recalled how he had walked close beside her, his hand hovering near her elbow, ready to catch her. How she had swayed, how he had reached out instinctively to—

But she just gently pushed his hand away. "I'm fine, Sam."

He remembered how her smile wavered as she closed her eyes to whisper her wish, how her hands trembled as she wrote it down and when the purple ribbon almost fell from her fingers. He tried to help—

But she shook her head. "I need to do this on my own."

She looped the ribbon around the lowest branch herself and her hand lingered there for a beat, as though she wasn't ready to let the wish go. Then she turned to Sam.

"Can you do something …" The words had caught in Elizabeth's throat, which she did her best to clear, "for me?"

He'd reached for her hand, his fingers closing over hers. "Of course. Anything."

"This wish—it needs time." A small smile touched her lips. "Promise you'll wait to read it? That you'll wait until your heart tells you it's time to come back?"

He fought to swallow the lump in his throat. "I promise," he'd said, though he hadn't written a wish of his own. Wishes couldn't give him what he truly needed—and deep down, he suspected they both knew it.

Now, standing on the porch, that promise—caught somewhere between a memory and a possibility—haunted him as much as the looming changes to Elizabeth's hometown.

Still, Sam felt something shift inside him as he considered Lisa's words. "Maybe I will."

3

Katie

"Katie, this letter ... it has to be a mistake." Emma's hand moved in small circles on Katie's back.

Katie blinked hard, trying to hold back the tears as her gaze drifted to the Wishing Tree. The ribbons shimmered under the fading sunlight, their colors softening to dusky gold. Below, wildflowers framed the base of the tree, purple coneflowers dissolved into shadows, and black-eyed Susans glowed like tiny embers at the edges.

"Look at me," Emma said, moving between Katie and the tree. "You've worked too hard for this. There's gotta be some sort of mix-up."

Katie's fingers clenched the paper, crumpling it, as if squeezing it tight might make the words disappear.

"Maybe I wasn't meant to—" Her voice cracked. She flattened the letter out, folded it, and tucked it into her pocket.

Emma squeezed Katie's arm, but before she could speak, her phone buzzed. There was a quick glance at the screen, then a huff. "It's Luke—something came up at the store. I'm so sorry, but I gotta go. You gonna be okay?"

Katie forced a smile. "Don't worry, Em. I'll be fine."

Emma hesitated, then crouched, cupping Benny's scruffy muzzle. "You take care of her, okay, Benny boy?"

Benny plopped down next to Katie, his tail thumping against the ground as if he had understood.

Straightening, Emma turned back to Katie and pulled her into a tight hug. "Promise you'll call if you need anything," she said. *"Anything."*

Katie leaned into her friend's shoulder and sniffled. "Promise."

Emma squeezed Katie's shoulders one last time, then flashed a quick smile before turning and hurrying down the cobblestone path.

Katie's hand moved to scratch behind Benny's ear, her gaze trailing Emma as she disappeared into the crowd, weaving between laughing families and flashing cameras. Then she released a shaky breath, lifting her eyes upward as the last streaks of sunlight bled into a twilight blue. Standing beneath the branches of the Wishing Tree, she knew it was time to add her own desperate wish to the hundreds already tied there.

She stepped up to the small wooden table beside the tree. Stacks of ribbons, blank tags, and seals sat waiting. Katie picked up a tag and smoothed the blue ribbon between her fingers, as if ironing out her own thoughts, while her chest rose and fell in long breaths. The enormity of her wish swirled in her mind ... The blank tag stared back at her ... Her fingers trembled slightly.

As she reached for the pen, the memory of opening day flashed through her mind—how she'd stood behind the counter arranging and rearranging the display of local authors, making sure everything was perfect. Her first customer had been a little girl who had saved her allowance to buy *The Secret Garden*. The joy on that child's face when Katie had gifted her a special bookmark still made her smile.

Katie swallowed hard and pressed her thumb against the ribbon. One deep breath, then another, but it wasn't enough to silence the nagging voice in her head.

Too late to fix the leaky roof.

Too late to find the funds for repairs.

Too late to save the one thing that has truly ever been mine.

Did it even matter? Wishes couldn't fix peeling paint or windows that stuck, no matter how hard she tried to open them. They also couldn't reignite the interest of a community lured away by big chain stores and online deals. And they certainly couldn't return the countless nights she'd spent on the shop floor, pouring her heart into events that no one showed up for.

A lump formed in her throat, but she pushed it down and wrote:

Please help me save my store.

Katie.

Carefully, she slid the tag into the seal, pressing down the edges to make sure her words were visible. Then she secured the tag to the ribbon, stretched up, and parting the branches ... She found the perfect spot.

There.

She tied it to the branch, and when she stepped back, she kept her eyes on the tag as it swayed among the others.

"Please, please, help me save my store," she whispered into the night.

The sight reminded her of the stories the townspeople swore were true—wishes granted beneath these very branches. Marriages blessed, illnesses cured, lost souls found ... Still, as she stood there, she couldn't help but wonder if it would happen for her—if her wish would come true.

A flicker of movement caught Katie's eye, and she turned.

A tall man stood a few steps away. There was something about the way he moved—or the reverent way he studied the tags? She noted how his silver-streaked hair caught the glow of the fairy lights as he carefully moved among the ribbons, and how that seemed at odds with his fingers as he traced each tag with a kind of urgency. Then there were his lips, mouthing the names or wishes written there. And every now and then ... His shoulders would tense when reading a particular tag, only to fall before moving on to the next.

Katie caught herself staring and spun back to face her own ribbon when Benny lunged. His excitement pulled Katie forward, tightening the leash against her wrist, sending her stumbling toward the man.

"Benny!"

But Benny had other ideas, letting out an enthusiastic "Ruff!" as he strained toward the stranger.

"That's a no-no, Benny." Katie tugged the leash as the man turned.

The stranger's eyes moved from Benny to her.

A blush crept over her cheeks. "Sorry if we bothered you."

"You're not a bother," he replied, smiling. "Seems like a good dog."

"He can be." Katie tucked back an imaginary strand of hair. "He is. He's just ... being weird, tonight."

The man chuckled. "Nah, he's just having fun."

"I guess." Katie felt her shoulders ease. "So, uhm, did you make a wish?"

"Not exactly," he said, rubbing the back of his neck. "But I'm looking for a ribbon—one someone else tied." He gestured toward the hundreds of ribbons on the tree. "Looking at all these though, I might need a wish to find it."

His laugh was soft, almost self-deprecating, but there was something deeper beneath it. Something like pain flickered across his face before he masked it with a smile. "I'm Sam, by the way." He held out his hand.

"Katie," she replied, meeting his hand with her own.

His palm was warm, his grip firm but gentle, and for a moment, it felt like neither of them wanted to let go.

When she pulled her hand back, she looked down at Benny, who nudged Sam's leg with his nose.

"Mind if I ...?" Sam was already crouching, hand outstretched.

"Oh, no. Go ahead," Katie said, smiling as Benny melted into Sam's touch.

"He's beautiful. What breed?"

"Miniature schnauzer. I adopted him two years ago from Second Chance Rescue here in town. Kept getting overlooked because of his age." She bit her bottom lip, then added, "I know what that's like. To be overlooked, I mean."

The moment the words slipped out, heat rushed to her cheeks.

Did I seriously just trauma dump?

She busied herself with the leash in her hands, keeping her eyes down before risking a peek at Sam, bracing for his reaction.

Sam's hand paused before continuing to stroke Benny's fur. "You can see it in his eyes—he's got a good soul. Dogs like him have been through a lot, but they still find a way to trust."

"You're right. It wasn't easy, though." She studied Benny's gray muzzle and cloudy eyes, thinking of the day she adopted him—how he had cowered in the corner of the kennel. "When I first brought him home, he wouldn't even look at me. I had to sit on the floor for hours to let him see I wasn't going anywhere." And now here he was, running up to a random man. A handsome man. Very handsome.

"Sounds like you gave him the second chance he deserved."

"He's the one who saved me."

Benny pressed into Sam as if he'd known him forever. "For the record, he's not usually this friendly with strangers. He must really like you."

Sam's lip curved into a smile as he looked up at her. "Well, I like you too—"

Katie's breath caught.

Did I hear him right?

"I mean, I like *him*. Not that I don't like you. Okay, you know what, uh …" Sam's ears turned red.

Katie laughed softly, still fiddling with Benny's leash.

As Sam stood, his eyes met hers in that slow way that made the cool evening air feel a little warmer. A flutter started in her stomach, spreading outward until even her fingertips tingled.

"Anyway, what about you, Katie? You think wishes really come true?"

4

Sam

Around them, kids darted past, clutching candy apples, while a local musician by the food trucks strummed his guitar. The air carried the sticky sweetness of fried dough and cinnamon, the same scents that had lingered two years ago when he had walked these paths with Elizabeth. Somehow, the memory turned the air sweeter and heavier all at once.

Sam exhaled a long, measured sigh, and when the tree lights caught in Katie's dark hair, his chest tightened.

"… I mean, I want to believe they do." Katie's gaze drifted to the Wishing Tree, where tiny lights tangled with the ribbons. "I need to believe they do, especially now. Sorry, I'm babbling."

"No need to apologize, it's all right." Sam watched Katie fidget with her pocket. "Everything okay?" The question escaped before he could stop it.

"Not really. I got this today." The faint tremor in her hands became more pronounced as she pulled out a piece of paper. "The building inspector cited my store code violations." She bit her bottom lip before pressing on. "And now, I have twenty-one days to fix everything or ..."

All the festival sounds faded to background noise. "Twenty-one days? That's barely any time at all."

"You're right, it's not." Katie zipped and unzipped her jacket pocket. "It's just ... I've tried so hard to keep up with all the things. It's an old building," she said, pointing toward Main Street. "But it's falling apart faster than I can fix it ..."

Sam shifted his weight and his hands slid into his pockets like they belonged there. "I'm in town for contract work. Renovation is kind of my thing. Might be able to help if you want me to swing by?"

What are you doing, Sam?

She looked up at him, and the smile blooming across her face made his breath catch. "You'd do that? For me?"

"Of course." He was already nodding, even as part of him screamed to walk away, to focus on what had brought him here in the first place.

Katie tugged her jacket tighter around her shoulders as Benny pressed against her legs.

Sam found himself envying how easily the old schnauzer could offer comfort without second-guessing every gesture.

"I don't want to impose—" Katie started.

"You're not." Sam caught himself staring at the way the lights shimmered in her brown eyes. She was the kind of pretty that ached, that made him want to look and keep looking.

Is this wrong? Even a little? Elizabeth's wish is tied to that tree, and here I am noticing another woman ...

He tried to push the thoughts away and cleared his throat. "Besides, your pal here," he nodded toward Benny, "already vouched for you."

"Yeah, I suppose he's a good judge of character." Katie kneeled to adjust Benny's collar. Before she could stand, the dog had already wandered to Sam and flopped onto his side, belly up.

Katie laughed. "Looks like you've got a fan."

Sam smiled, rubbing his hand across Benny's belly as the dog's legs flailed in a blur of unrestrained joy. "Clearly, I'm his favorite now."

When he stood up, Katie tilted her head to look up at him, and—

His words felt too big for his mouth.

So, he took a breath. "Hey—" A couple strolled by with a toddler. Sam hadn't planned to ask, but the words slipped out anyway. "Have you, uhm, eaten? Because if not, I figured we can grab a bite while we talk about what repairs need to be done."

"Oh, I—" She seemed to search his face for something, and Sam wondered what she saw there.

He thought about his string of awkward, half-hearted attempts at dating after Elizabeth's passing. Like the lunch where his date stared at her phone the entire time, stopping occasionally to photograph her untouched salad. Or the yoga instructor—set up by a friend—who "forgot" her wallet and ordered the most expensive items on the menu; it didn't help he had spotted her running the same scheme with another guy at the same restaurant a week later. The final straw had been the marketing executive who spent their entire coffee date taking loud business calls, pausing just long enough to tell him she "usually dated taller men."

How is 6'2" not tall enough?

Back then, Sam believed the hardest part of moving on would be taking the first step—putting himself back out there, trying to date again. But forgiving himself for wanting to move on—that had been the hardest part. Sometimes, it still was ...

He pushed the memories aside and focused on Katie. This wasn't like those failed dates. There was no pretense here, no forced small talk. Just her and Benny and a conversation that already felt different.

Wait, this isn't a date. Right?

Either way, he knew he was in trouble—caring when he shouldn't, noticing what he couldn't ignore, feeling more than he dared admit. He tried to keep his face neutral, casual, but when Katie's eyes met his, he felt exposed.

"I, uhm ..." Benny nudged Katie's leg, as if urging her forward. She finally released a breath, a smile, a shrug. "You know what? I could use some carbs right about now. I've even got the perfect place in mind."

Sam smiled, his chest feeling lighter than it had in years. "Lead the way."

As they walked away from the Wishing Tree, Sam glanced back at the branches. Somewhere up there, Elizabeth's last wish waited for him, but he would have to come back later. Because for the first time in a long while, he wondered if something other than grief might be waiting for him.

5

Katie

Katie reached for the door handle, but Sam stepped ahead and opened it for her. It was a small gesture, the sort she hadn't realized she had missed until now.

As they entered Phil's Diner, a blast of warm air brushed her face, carrying the comforting aroma of waffles and hash browns that had welcomed her over the years. The jukebox hummed with a Taylor Swift tune, while teenagers clustered at the counter, sharing fries and gossip. Faded scuff marks on the checkered floor told stories of countless footsteps to the booths. The same old photos lined the walls—Phil's dad on opening day, the high school football team's championship win, and a snapshot of the Second Chance Rescue event where Phil's food truck served free pie and lemonade.

"Well, well, well! Look who decided to grace us with her presence!" Phil's voice boomed. He emerged from behind the counter in his signature stance—arms crossed over an apron spotted in grease stains and flour, with a dish towel draped over his shoulder. "Started to think you'd forgotten about us, stranger."

Katie winced. Avoiding this place hadn't been intentional—like missing movie nights with Emma or letting her yoga mat collect dust. Lately, it felt easier to hide in her store than face anyone. Her books didn't ask questions she couldn't answer. "Sorry, Phil. Been busy."

The diner's golden light caught the grays creeping into his red beard—*When had that happened?*

"Life doesn't slow down for us business owners, does it?" Phil's gaze shifted past her, landing on Sam with a curious gleam. "And who's this?" His eyes lit up like Emma's did whenever she was about to mention her husband's latest single friend who'd "be perfect for you, Katie."

Great.

The last guy she had been set up with had spent the entire dinner bragging about his investment portfolio and how he only flew first class.

"Sam." He reached out to shake Phil's hand.

Phil's hand met his. "Any friend of Katie's is always welcome. Let's get you folks settled."

Katie followed Phil to the booth by the window, where she could still see the festival lights. Benny leaped onto the seat beside her, claiming it with the confidence of someone who clearly owned the place.

Phil glanced at Benny. "And there's my favorite customer. Still keeping your momma in line? Lord knows someone has to." He then pulled out his notepad and turned his attention to Katie. "The usual? Lemon poppy seed pancakes with blueberry syrup?"

Her stomach growled, but before she could speak, Derek's voice slithered into her mind.

Should you be eating that?

Those jeans are getting pretty tight, don't you think?

Followed by: *Why are you upset? Just giving a helpful suggestion.*

Katie crossed her arms over her stomach. "I'll take a side salad and water, thanks."

She caught Phil's frown, but all he said was, "Will do."

Great, now I'm a disappointment to Phil too.

He had been there through everything—her move to town from Ohio, the mess with Derek, the way she'd slowly disappeared into herself ... He had even offered to "have a word" with Derek after the divorce, though she'd talked him out of it.

Phil turned to Sam. "And for you, good sir?"

"Beyond burger with avocado and peppers." Sam looked up from his menu. "Also, fries and a water. Thanks."

"Coming right up, y'all!" Phil stuck his pencil behind his ear and headed to the kitchen. On his way, he flipped the *Reserved* sign on the next booth. Classic Phil, always looking out for her without making a big deal about it.

The fan whirred overhead while Katie traced invisible circles on the table with her fingertip.

"So, what kind of business do you run, and what exactly are those violations?" Sam asked.

Katie pulled out the letter and unfolded it on the table. "A bookstore." She slid it toward him. "Brace yourself—it's a lot."

She watched as Sam picked up the letter and read over the violations. Then he paused, looked toward the window, and then back at the letter. For a moment, he seemed to forget where he was, but why?

When he cleared his throat, Katie felt heat rise in her cheeks, realizing she must have been staring. Chewing on the inside of her lip, she finally asked, "Well?"

"Well," he began, "water damage, mold, outdated wiring ..." His voice trailed off as he glanced at her. "This is a nightmare."

Katie groaned. "It's the worst," she muttered, reaching for a sugar packet from the dispenser and fiddling with it. "Mold near the shelves? That's news to me. Wiring? Sure, it's old, but I've never had a problem with it—until now."

Sam's brows lifted as he read further. "Yeah, but support beams. Now, that's serious. Have you seen anything unusual—sagging floors, cracks, anything like that?"

"The floors have been uneven for a while," she admitted.

He leaned back and tapped his chin. "What's the deal with the plumbing?"

"That's from the gutters," she explained, leaning back in the booth. "They've been clogged forever. I kept the shop in the divorce, and my ex got the house. Fixing things was supposed to be part of the deal, but—" She shrugged. "You know how that goes."

"He got the house?" Sam raised a brow. "So, where do you live?"

Katie hesitated for a beat before answering. "I've got an apartment above the bookstore. It's not fancy, but it works—or at least it used to." She looked down at the table, organizing the sweetener packets by color. "If I lose the store, I lose the apartment too." Her voice dropped to a whisper. "My home."

A pause hung between them, and Katie braced herself for a dismissive comment or a suggestion to hire someone and move on. That's what Derek would've done.

Sam leaned in. "We'll figure this out, okay? Let's prioritize. What's the biggest issue?"

Katie blinked. No interrupting, no eye-rolling, no quick fixes like Derek used to toss at her before going back to his phone?

No, Sam's eyes had stayed on her face when she spoke, as if her next word might be too important to miss. In fact, he even asked questions that showed he was really hearing her, not just waiting for his turn to talk.

Huh. He's not just listening—he's helping.

When Phil returned with their food and drinks—he had something extra. "Almost forgot—special delivery for the gentleman here." He set a bag of Riley's Recipe Sweet Potato Chews on the table. "Emma dropped these off last week. The latest flavor from Barking Orders. Anyway, I'll leave y'all to it. Enjoy."

"Thank you," Katie and Sam said in unison. They smiled at each other before turning to Phil, who gave a nod before heading to the kitchen.

Benny perked up as Katie opened the bag and handed over a treat. He took it carefully, settled on the booth seat, and began gnawing away while keeping an eye on Katie's bowl—just in case she decided to share.

"Back to your question," she said, spearing a cherry

tomato with her fork. "The biggest issue is this entire situation. When the inspector came by last month, he barely looked around. Said everything was fine, and that I should patch up what I could. But this?" She waved her fork at the letter. "Complete one-eighty. It's like he visited two different buildings."

"Hmm ... Did he say anything else that seemed off?" Sam dipped a fry into ketchup.

Katie thought back, trying to piece together the memory. "Nothing specific, but during the first inspection, before our grand opening, he wrote everything down and explained each requirement. Very thorough. This time, though, he didn't write anything down and kept checking his phone like his mind was somewhere else. Oh, and he practically ran out the door afterward."

"That's weird." Sam wiped his mouth. "How about I come by tomorrow? Sometimes a fresh set of eyes helps."

Katie picked at her salad, trying not to let her thoughts wander. But there was something in Sam's eyes—something that said he really cared. For a split second, her gaze lingered on the tattoos winding across his forearms—the shapes and lines piqued her curiosity.

Not now, Katie.

She exhaled quietly and then offered a smile. "Tomorrow? That'd be amazing." She hadn't meant to sound so hopeful. But after having spent so long handling everything herself, help felt ... strange. Good strange, but strange all the same. She straightened in her seat, then forced her shoulders to relax. "The shop's off Main Street, across from—"

"Katie? Katie Hayes? Is that you?"

Her fork clattered against the bowl as Benny's head jerked up beside her. That voice—too familiar. The kind that made her wish the vinyl booth could swallow her whole.

6

Sam

Katie stiffened at the sound of the voice behind them.

"Ada!" Katie's tone shot up. "How are you?"

The lively chatter of the diner softened as an elderly woman shuffled to their booth, squinting through powder-blue glasses that matched her sweater. Her eyes bounced between them with a sly twinkle. "I didn't know you were dating again, dear."

Katie's cheeks flushed. "Oh no, we're not... I mean, Sam's only—"

"A friend," Sam interjected, leaning forward a bit, like he could somehow shield her from Ada's sharp gaze. "Actually, we just met tonight."

"Oh, honey, that's how it always starts." Ada's red-stained lips curved into a knowing smile. "Take Frank and me. Many moons ago, we were just study partners in chemistry. But let me tell you something about chemistry—"

Katie's hands moved to her face, but Sam still caught the soft, breathy laugh by the lift in her shoulders.

Beside her, Benny pressed closer, as if more socially attuned than some people.

"But speaking of news—" Ada's voice dipped as she leaned in, flooding Sam's nose with flowery perfume—the kind his grandmother used to wear. "Have you heard about these development plans for our town? It's all over the Facebook how these carpetbaggers want to turn our town into a resort nightmare. Bless their hearts, they just don't know better." She clicked her tongue, casting a wary glance around the diner as if someone might overhear. "And with the pressure from city hall, not to mention your ex—"

Katie's face went pale. "Derek? What's he got to do with anything?"

Derek?

Sam's stomach twisted, and his eyes fixed on a water ring on the table.

"Oh, Derek Huntington's knee-deep in all of it." Ada fussed with her wild silver hair. "He's been the one buying up everything downtown."

"Huntington," Sam muttered. Saying it aloud left a bitter taste in his mouth.

Ada's glasses slid down her nose as she leaned in closer. "Word is they're planning to tear down half of Main Street and most of the boardwalk. Can you imagine?" She shook her head, earrings swaying. "My Daddy, God rest his soul, would roll over in his grave."

Before they could react, Ada swept them into a hug.

The heavy floral scent made Sam dizzy, but he caught

Katie's gaze over Ada's shoulder—a moment that lingered too long. He looked away, toward the ceiling fan, which now seemed fascinating.

"You two lovebirds take care now." Ada released them and sashayed away, her dress swishing around her ankles, like she was exiting stage left. Half the diner turned to watch, but she just sailed past, head held high, leaving a cloud of perfume and whispers in her wake.

"That's Ada for you. Part historian, part matchmaker, full-time gossiper." Katie's forced smile had faltered.

Sam nodded. "She's quite something," he said, as his mind spun with the name Ada had just dropped.

Derek Huntington is Katie's ex?

The Derek who'd ditched her and the bookshop?

The same Derek who'd hired me to—

Each realization hit harder than the last until he could barely breathe around the truth of it.

"Should we head out?" Katie was already on her feet, zipping her jacket as Benny hopped down from the booth.

Sam blinked himself back into the moment. "Yeah, good idea."

As he reached for his wallet, Katie pulled out a few bills from her bag. "Let me get this."

He held up a hand. "No, no. I've got it."

"Are you sure?" Her head tilted. "I don't mind splitting it."

The thought of his nearly empty bank account flashed through his head, but he pushed it aside. "It's all good. My treat."

Katie paused before giving a hesitant smile. "Thanks."

He left enough cash for dinner and a solid tip, catching Phil's eye as they headed for the door. The diner owner gave him a look that was equal parts approval and warning—an unspoken message: *Don't mess this up, son.*

The door chimed when they stepped into the cool night air, tinged with caramel, cinnamon, and wood smoke. Festival lights blurred in the distance as Benny's paws pattered along the cobblestones.

Sam's stomach churned as one name continued to echo through his thoughts:

Derek Huntington.

Katie's ex. The developer. The same man who had signed his checks. The connections tightened like a noose.

His thoughts escaped to Elizabeth, like they always did when he felt cornered.

What would she have thought of tonight? Of me, here with Katie, like this? Of what I've gotten myself into with Derek?

The evening hadn't been a date—not really—but it had felt … effortless. Though, in a way that only amplified his guilt. Sam slowed his stride to match Katie's, anchoring himself in her voice to drown out the panic clawing at his chest. He grinned as she launched into a story about an interaction with a customer.

"… and I swear, he insisted he could return the book because he didn't like it, even though he'd read the whole thing."

"At least he didn't try to argue about store credit," Sam

said, remembering his retail stint back in high school.

"Oh, he did that too. For twenty minutes." Katie's laugh carried on the evening air. "Two years running this place, and people still find new ways to ..." Her voice trailed off as they turned the corner away from Main Street.

He hadn't realized how far they'd walked until Katie stopped beside a narrow staircase leading up to a brick building.

"All right, we're here," Katie said.

As the brick building came into full view, the sight punched the air from Sam's lungs. His chest constricted as memories flooded back—the iron sign posts where Elizabeth's hand-painted sign had once hung. The brass door handle she'd polished the day they got the keys. The display window where she sketched seasonal events ...

"Sam, you okay?"

He barely heard Katie's voice over the roar of his pulse. Two years of avoiding this street, and now, here he was, standing in the exact spot where they'd taken their photo after the lawyer handed them the deed. Elizabeth's grandmother's legacy—the bookstore that she had dreamed of running since she was a child. It was supposed to be their future.

"Yeah, just ..." His throat felt dry. "Good location."

"It is, isn't it?" She gestured to her gray Corolla, its back windshield plastered with stickers. "Need a ride back to the inn? I don't mind."

A streetlight flickered overhead, and for a second, the shadows made her look just like—but no. She was Katie. Just Katie. And that was enough to terrify him. He couldn't get the words out fast enough. "No, thanks. I could use the walk."

"Well, thanks for dinner," Katie said, slipping her free hand into her jacket pocket. "And for offering to help with the shop. You really don't have to—"

"I want to." He surprised himself with how much he wanted to. Despite everything with Derek, despite Elizabeth's wish still waiting on the Wishing Tree, despite standing in front of the building they'd had to sell to pay for treatments that hadn't even saved her—he'd said he would help.

And he would.

Somehow.

Katie looked up at him, and something in her expression made his chest ache. The wind teased her hair, and Sam shoved his hands in his pockets, resisting the urge to brush it back.

"See you tomorrow?" he asked.

"Can't wait!" Her eyes widened, like she hadn't meant to say it that loud. She turned toward the door, Benny's leash wrapped loosely around one hand as she fumbled with her keys in the other. The metal jingled as she missed the lock once, then twice, before finally sliding the key in with a quiet click.

Sam watched Katie and Benny vanish into the store—into Elizabeth's store—feeling like the ground was crumbling beneath his feet. The same brass bell chimed as the door closed, the one Elizabeth had picked out from that antique shop in Savannah. He could still hear her voice: *I know it's silly, but doesn't it sound like home? It's perfect, Sam.*

He waited until Katie's lights flicked on upstairs, then started the long walk back to the Sandy Shores Inn. The brass bell's chime seemed to linger, trailing behind him down the cobblestone street—guiding him through the divide between what was and what could be, between holding on and letting go. When he finally reached the porch of the inn, his phone buzzed in his pocket.

> **Derek:** *We need to start the project earlier than expected. Tomorrow. Need you to call first thing in the morning.*

Tomorrow?

Sam stared at the screen until it dimmed and then slipped the phone into his pocket. Leaning against the porch rail, he released a sigh, knowing there wouldn't be any sleep tonight.

Tomorrow he would have to walk through that door again, past the wall where Elizabeth had been so excited to paint her favorite book quotes, under the skylight she'd planned to put a reading nook beneath. Tomorrow he would have to help Katie fix up the place he and Elizabeth had been forced to sell when the medical bills had drained everything they had. Or—

Tomorrow he'd have to choose which commitment to break: Finding Elizabeth's last wish on the Wishing Tree, his promise to Katie, or the contract with Derek.

7

Katie

Friday

Katie stared at her bedroom ceiling, counting popcorn bumps for the second time since waking up. Her alarm wouldn't buzz for another half-hour, but her thoughts were already running on a loop: the inspection notice, dinner at Phil's, and Sam. Mostly Sam.

Benny's snores and occasional dream barks filled the room.

Katie glanced at him sprawled across his Serta Orthopedic bed by the nightstand. She'd spent more on it than she cared to admit, but it was a splurge she didn't regret. Watching him stretch luxuriously on the high-density foam, she was sure he had struck the jackpot compared to her lumpy, college-era mattress.

Outside her window, the sky had lightened to a muted

pre-dawn gray that made everything look a little sad. When her alarm finally buzzed, she smacked it and sat up.

"Morning, buddy." She looked down at Benny. His tail thumped against the edge of his bed, and when her feet hit the cold floor, he gave a low grunt and rolled onto his back, paws splayed in the air like he was determined to stay put.

Katie chuckled and leaned over to scratch his belly. "You wanna sleep in, huh?" She shook her head. "Yeah, same. But one of us has to act like an adult around here."

Moving about to get ready for the day, she threw on her running shoes and grabbed a hoodie that may or may not have come from the lost and found box. The tag was too faded to tell, and no one had claimed it in months, so technically it was hers now.

That's how lost and founds work, right?

She sighed, reaching for Benny's harness hanging on the corner of her nightstand, and looked back to her adorable old pup. "All right, you've snoozed long enough. Come on. We've got things to do, so let's get moving."

Benny made no move to get up. Just stared her down.

"Don't give me that look." She bent down and slipped the harness over his head.

Benny huffed dramatically but didn't resist as she buckled it into place. "You know the drill."

The back stairs creaked beneath them as they made their way down for their morning beach walk. Maybe the ocean air would clear her head? Usually, the beach was her reset button—even on days when her thoughts felt tangled beyond repair.

A gust had whipped off the water and bit through her

clothes, making her tuck her free hand into her pocket. She paused, glancing down at her sneakers and thin socks, wishing she'd dressed warmer.

So much for that reset.

The beach unfolded ahead, empty except for the usual early morning crowd: Jan power walking with her greyhound rescue, Old Pete collecting shells for his grandkids, and the guy with the black lab who always wore neon-green running shorts no matter the weather. This was her favorite time of day, before the tourists descended, when Hadley Cove still felt like it belonged to them. Just the locals, sharing nods as they passed, their footprints mixing in the sand until you couldn't tell whose was whose.

Katie remembered what Old Pete had told her that first winter after she'd moved here: "This town's got good bones, Katie-girl. Just needs the right people to love it." He'd been sorting through his morning's shell collection, showing her how to spot the unbroken sand dollars beneath the foam.

Another bitter wind swept across the beach, stinging her cheeks until she yanked her hoodie strings tight. Beside her, Benny meandered through the sand, stopping to investigate every smell.

Katie caught the slight hitch in Benny's step. His arthritis always seemed worse in the cold. "Just a quick lap today, old man. We've got stuff to do."

Back in her apartment, Katie measured out Benny's breakfast while he supervised, head tilted like she might mess up the same routine they'd done for two years.

The coffee maker gurgled to life while she rummaged through her cabinets, finding nothing but a stale protein bar and a half-empty bag of chips for herself. Grocery shopping had fallen off her to-do list—along with getting her car serviced, fixing the dripping bathroom faucet, and basically anything else that cost money.

The pile of bills on her counter told a clear story. Electric was two weeks past due. The water bill glared with its red *FINAL NOTICE* stamp she'd been ignoring, and she didn't dare look at her health insurance premiums. Rotating which utilities to short each month in a game of musical chairs had caught up to her.

Katie ran the numbers again, like maybe they would be different this time. Even if she didn't pay herself for another month, cut back on ordering new releases, and survived on ramen noodles, she'd still come up short. And now with these repairs? Her credit score was decent—maybe Lighthouse Community Bank would consider a small business loan, since Harbor Trust Bank had already turned her down over the summer. Or she could appeal to the Bank of Mom and Dad—low interest rates, flexible payment plans, and a judgmental sigh, then the inevitable lecture, all included at no extra charge.

No, no, no.

She had already borrowed from them twice since the divorce and would auction off her entire vintage Jane Austen collection before she put herself through that again.

She shoved the pile and the thoughts that came with it

away for Future Katie to handle. Her hands shook slightly as she crammed the stack of bills under *Gordon Ramsay's Home Cooking*, which was propped up at an angle that would probably earn her one of his famous kitchen meltdowns. Just looking at the pile caused her to close her eyes as she willed herself not to cry. There wasn't room for that today. Not yet. Present Katie needed to make herself presentable—for Sam.

Katie walked over and stared into her closet, fighting what felt like an existential crisis. As she pushed hangers back and forth, each scrape against the metal rod made her a little more frantic than the last.

This shouldn't be hard. He's just coming by to look at things. That's all.

Even so, she found herself reaching for her red sweater—the one that actually fit right—and her good jeans, the pair that always made her feel more confident. Usually, she saved them for the rare occasions when Emma insisted on dragging her out somewhere nice.

Twenty minutes and two attempts at eyeliner later, she gave herself a final once-over in the mirror. Not that she cared what she looked like. This was strictly professional. Though some tinted lip balm wouldn't hurt.

"Come on, Benny." She grabbed her keys from the wooden hand-painted hanger by the door, with the word *home* etched into it.

Benny eased himself from his corner bed with a stretch and a yawn that showed all his teeth.

She double-checked the deadbolt, then triple-checked it before following him into the narrow stairwell.

Downstairs, Katie flitted around the store as if she'd had three shots of espresso instead of her usual coffee. She straightened books that were already straight, dusted shelves she had dusted yesterday, and wiped down spotless counters. It wasn't until she caught her reflection in the storefront window, circling the same table for the third time in fifteen minutes, that she realized Benny was watching her from his corner bed, probably judging her.

Katie turned to Benny. "Don't look at me like that." She held up some throw pillows she had found in storage. "Now, blue or red?"

He blinked at her, unbothered.

"Thanks for the input. Super helpful." She decided to use them both, before heading over to unlock the door and flip the *Closed* sign to *Open*.

The wall clock read 10:10 a.m. No customers yet—not exactly unusual lately, but still. Her sales tracker didn't lie. She was facing a steady six-month decline. Last Tuesday: zero sales. Wednesday: one paperback and a bookmark. Thursday through Sunday: only a trickle of foot traffic, mostly browsers who left empty-handed.

Meanwhile, the big chain store in the next town over wasn't helping, with its fancy cafe and corporate buying power. Weekend story times, monthly book clubs, and celebrity author signings—they had it all. Then there was Amazon, with its endless inventory and next-day delivery.

Her regulars were disappearing one by one. Mrs. Chen,

who used to come in every Tuesday for her romance novels, now had a Kindle. The high school kids, who would hang out in the teen section after school, had migrated to the chain store's "study cafe," complete with plush chairs and the fastest Wi-Fi in existence.

And Katie had tried to set herself apart from the competition with wholesome activities like the pumpkin decorating contest at last year's fall event, Cozy Chapters & Cider, which had brought in decent sales. However, this year, she had barely gotten any RSVPs.

Katie's eyes drifted to the Fall Book Festival display in the window. It looked … sad—like it couldn't decide if it was trying too hard or not hard enough. She should have put up more flyers, or at least learned how to make graphics that didn't scream, "I just discovered Canva." Maybe she should've spent more on advertising instead of fixing that leak in the storage room. But then again, moldy books wouldn't exactly help business either.

That's when the words *immediate attention required* glared at her from the letter in her periphery. She plucked it from the cluttered desk, where it perched on top of receipts and sticky notes, and dialed the number.

Her phone felt like a five-pound weight in her hand, each ring tightening the knot in her stomach.

"Hadley Cove City Hall, how may I direct your call?"

"Yes, I need to speak with Raymond Barnes about a building inspection."

"Mr. Barnes is out of the office today. Would you like to leave a message?"

Katie's fingers tapped against the counter. "Yes, please.

This is Katie Hayes from Breezy Tails Bookshop. It's about the inspection notice—it's urgent. I think there's been some kind of mistake."

"One moment, please." The sound of typing clicked through the line. "And how can he reach you, Ms. Hayes?"

Katie rattled off her number, then added, "I'll be at the shop all day."

"I'll make sure he gets the message as soon as he returns to the office," the receptionist said.

"Thanks. Appreciate you," Katie said, hanging up her phone when the bell jingled above the door.

Emma breezed in with Riley straining at his leash. She then glanced around the empty store before unclipping it and setting him free.

The golden retriever bolted toward Benny, and within seconds, both dogs were zooming around the mystery section. They had their own routine—three laps around the shelf, pause to bark at each other, then another two laps just because.

"Well, they're at it again," Katie said with a small smile, watching the dogs race around.

A few paperbacks hit the floor as Riley's tail caught the bottom shelf. But honestly? At least someone was excited to be in her store.

"Riley, sit!" Emma laughed, not sounding particularly committed to the command. She turned her attention to Katie and, with a squint, gave the woman an exaggerated once-over. "Okay, who are you and what have you done with my friend who lives in oversized hoodies?"

Heat crept up Katie's neck. "What? Can't a girl dress up

every once in a while?"

"Uh-huh." Emma leaned on the counter. "How you holding up after yesterday?"

"Better, I think." Katie fidgeted with the display cards by the register. "I tried calling the inspector, but he's out. Oh, and someone I met at the festival is coming by to look at the violations today."

Emma's eyebrows shot up. "Someone? Is that why you're wearing your good sweater?"

"This isn't—" Katie tugged at the hem. "Fine. Maybe. We had dinner at Phil's last night."

"What! And you're just mentioning this now? Spill. Immediately." Emma's grin turned dangerous. "Is he tall, dark, and handsome? Or are we talking sweet, guy-next-door vibes?"

The bell chimed again, and Katie felt a jolt shoot through her bones. She didn't need to look up to know who it was—maybe because her good sweater suddenly felt too warm, too obvious, too everything …

8

Sam

THE SMART MOVE WOULD'VE been to turn back, call Derek, and take the money—just a simple job to clear his debts and pay Elizabeth's hospital bills. Instead, he took another step forward and the scents of aged paper and polished wood carried him into a world that once felt like home.

He shook his head, adjusting the tool belt slung over his hip.

Pull it together, Sam.

But he couldn't. The sunlight that streamed through the windows kept his head in a lucid daydream as all of Elizabeth's hopes revisited him in what felt like an alternate reality. The vintage iron ceiling fan he remembered still hung overhead. A stack of donated books, his past love would have approved of, sat in an overfilled wicker basket by the door. And at the counter—

Would she approve of this? Of her?

Katie stood beside a redheaded middle-aged woman,

their focus on Benny and a golden retriever weaving through the aisles—at least until he entered the room.

The redhead extended her hand with a smile. "Hey, I'm Emma."

"Sam." He returned the handshake.

"Nice to meet you, but I hear you and Katie have a lot to do, so I won't keep y'all." Emma's attention turned back to the golden retriever, and she whistled. "Come on, Riley. Time to go." As she clipped on his leash, she turned to Katie with an exaggerated wink and spoke loud enough that Sam couldn't miss it: "Silver fox."

Katie's eyes widened as she shot Emma a knowing look.

Sam bit back a grin. It wasn't the worst thing he had been called, and the nickname wasn't entirely off the mark. His salt-and-pepper hair had drawn its share of compliments, though he rarely thought about it. Perhaps because the grays that had accumulated were evidence of the years he'd lived through—not all of them easy.

"Have fun, y'all," Emma called out. The bell jingled as she left Sam alone with Katie—or almost. Benny padded over, resting his chin on Sam's boot.

Sam crouched beside the old miniature schnauzer, but his eyes continued to wander the store. His gaze settled on the spots where Elizabeth had once sketched out her plans.

The window nook where she'd planned to put cushions. "Blue ones, Sam. But not navy blue. More like the ocean on a clear day."

The corner she had wanted for story time, where she'd described the mural she imagined. "Forest animals, but whimsical ones. As if they just walked out of a fairy tale."

When he looked up, Katie was watching him.

She'd done something different today—makeup that drew him to her sweet brown eyes, hair pulled back in a way that framed the soft curves of her jaw, accentuated her neck, and made him notice things he shouldn't. Those fitted jeans didn't hurt either. He stood quickly, shoving those thoughts where they belonged—in the "not happening" box.

Katie patted her thigh as she coaxed Benny. "Come on, boy. To your spot," she said, nodding toward the dog bed nestled in the corner.

Benny tilted his head for a moment before trotting over and curling into it.

Katie stood and held out a letter with a wry smile. "So, ready to break my heart?"

Sam smiled. "I would never."

"I hope not." Something flickered across Katie's face—relief, maybe something more? She looked down at the paper in her hands, then handed it to Sam. "Follow me."

They began at the front of the store as Sam held the inspector's letter like a checklist. He tapped the first item with his pencil. "Water damage. Where's that supposed to be?"

Katie gestured toward the wall near the shelves. "Here. He claimed there's mold."

Sam tucked the pencil behind his ear, pulled a small flashlight from his tool belt, and clicked it on. Angling the beam along the wall, he ran his hand over the surface and inspected the baseboards. The paint was peeling slightly, but nothing more.

He then crouched down and shined the light into the

corners where the wall met the floor. "No visible mold."

He straightened and sniffed the air. "No smell."

Turning back to Katie as he turned off his flashlight, he said, "Maybe needs a little sanding and fresh paint. But not a health risk."

Katie exhaled. "Exactly! Next?"

Sam let out a soft laugh, then scanned the paper. "Electrical hazards?"

She led him to an outlet by the mystery section, plugged a lamp into it, and jiggled the cord until the light flickered on. "Quirky, but it works."

Sam reached into another pocket on his tool belt, retrieving a small screwdriver. He popped off the cover plate and inspected the wires. "Copper wiring. Probably from the '70s. Not dangerous, just dated."

"Thank goodness," Katie muttered. "I knew I wasn't crazy. This place has its problems, but not as bad as the letter made it sound."

He jotted a note in the margin before glancing at the next item. "Foundation issues?"

"In the storage room." She led the way down the hall.

Sam's attention caught on the wall, covered with framed photos of community events. The first photo was of a Halloween party with kids beaming beside their favorite literary characters. Next to it, a man dressed as Sherlock Holmes, reading to wide-eyed children. There was even a *Pride and Prejudice* tea party where everyone wore period costumes, the women in empire-waist dresses and the men in tailcoats.

"Those are from our costume events," Katie said with a

smile. "They always bring out the biggest crowds. Something magical happens when people step into their favorite characters."

Sam moved closer to study the pictures, trying to ignore how aware he was of Katie's presence beside him. As her arm brushed his, she turned back down the hall. "Come on, the storage room's this way."

Sam followed, his thoughts still caught between the photos on the wall and how Katie lit up when she talked about them.

Inside, the room was packed with boxes, outdated racks, and shelves holding a jumble of items. Katie pointed toward a crack in the ceiling, turning just as Sam stepped closer. They bumped into each other in the dim light and her hand landed on his chest. He could feel the warmth of her palm through his thin work shirt. It sent his pulse racing.

She glanced at her splayed fingers on his shirt. "Sorry, I—"

For a moment, neither of them moved.

Time seemed to slow, trapped in a bubble created by that small space.

Captivated by her dark eyes and the slight part of her lips, Sam caught himself leaning in, his hand drifting up, almost of its own accord ...

But then his breath caught as his gaze landed on the framed photo beside her.

Is that—?

He took a side step and reached for it, removing it from the shelf.

A gap-toothed little girl, tucked snugly in what looked

like her grandmother's lap, grinned back at him.

Elizabeth ...

Sam remembered the night she had shown him this same photo on their couch after a long day of house hunting.

"This was where I fell in love with books," Elizabeth had told him, touching her grandmother's face so gently. "Where I learned stories were magic. Gran would let me help her sort through the new arrivals, and I'd always sneak my favorites to that corner by the window. Used to say I'd do the same thing someday—share that magic with other kids."

"Sam?" Katie's voice broke through the haze. "You okay?"

"Yeah ... Just thinking about this." He handed the framed photo back to her.

"I see." Katie took the picture back and placed it back in its spot, exactly as it had been found. "Well, it's been here since I opened. Guess I just never had the heart to take it down. Do you know either of—"

Tap. Tap.

Sam paused, his attention having shifted to the support beam in the corner, which made a hollow sound when he tapped it again with his knuckles. He pressed a screwdriver into the wood. It sank slightly. It was spongier than it should have been.

Not good, but fixable.

Keeping the concern to himself, he said, "We're good for now." Katie had enough to worry about.

As he stepped out of the storage room, Katie followed closely.

Pulling the door shut behind her, she asked, "So, what's

next?"

"We need to talk to that building inspector."

"Actually, I reached out this morning. But he wasn't there, so I left him a message." She licked her lips. "But at least that ball is already in motion."

"Yes, it's a good start, very proactive of you," Sam said with a warm smile.

She smiled back, and it was nice to see her confidence soar in the moment, even as he began mentally sorting through what needed immediate attention. Anything to keep his mind occupied and not enchanted by her.

He swallowed hard. "I'll draft some plans tonight and bring them by tomorrow. See what we can tackle right away."

Katie threw her arms around him. "Thank you!"

He stiffened.

She stepped back quickly, clearing her throat. Her eyes flickered to the floor, then back up to his. "Sorry, I just—I thought I was gonna have to handle all of this"—she gestured around to the store before her arms flopped down to her side—"alone."

"Don't be sorry." His skin still tingled where she had touched him.

Katie gave a small nod, bit her bottom lip, and then seemed to remember something. "Oh, and we have an event here in the morning." She fiddled with her sleeve. "So, I was thinking that maybe ..." She sighed. "That maybe I should tell everyone we might be closing. I mean, it feels wrong to let people place orders if we might not be here to fill them."

Sam wanted to reassure her, to say she was jumping the gun, that they'd figure it out ... but the look in her eyes stopped him. Because what if they couldn't save the store? He didn't want to make a promise that he couldn't keep. So instead, he asked, "Need an extra hand? I can swing by, help out. Maybe tackle some repairs while we're at it."

"You sure? You'd really do that?" Her voice stirred something in his chest that hadn't moved for months.

"Yeah, of course. I'll be here."

Buzz ... Buzz ...

His hand instinctively went to the pocket his phone was in.

Gotta be Derek.

"I should go." Sam backed toward the front door, needing air. Space. Time to think. "But tomorrow?"

"Tomorrow."

Sam stepped out into the late afternoon sun and checked his phone as he climbed into his truck. He was right. Four missed calls and a voicemail from the man of the hour himself.

Can't avoid him forever.

Ignoring the voicemail, he pressed the call button ...

Derek answered on the first ring. "Where in the world have you been?"

"Had some personal stuff to handle."

"Well, I hope you figured it out because I need you to listen and listen close. The blueprints for the new Hadley Cove development are done, and it's already been preapproved by the city, pending review. That's where you come in, Sammy boy. I need you to go over the architect's plans and make sure everything checks out, *today*. Also, make sure you visit the demolition sites and verify the numbers. We'll be starting with the old hardware store on Fifth and moving down the block. That bookstore at the end of Main will be—"

A knot tightened in Sam's stomach. "I'm done, Derek. Find someone else."

"Done? What do you mean, 'Done'? We haven't even started!"

"The project. I'm out. I'll pay back what you fronted me, but I'm done."

"You can't just—"

Sam smashed *End Call* with his thumb and stuffed the phone into his pocket.

What have I done?

Turning down Derek's offer meant more than just losing a paycheck. It meant choosing uncertainty over security, hope over practicality. The money from this job would've covered bills through spring and paid off the last of Elizabeth's hospital debt, which still showed up every month like clockwork. But seeing Katie's face light up when he offered to help? That was worth more than Derek's blood money.

Now what?

Sam's hand moved to his chin as he did some mental math. His bills were covered until November. After that? Odd jobs could get him through, and skipping coffee runs wouldn't hurt. Also, the credit card could float him for a while.

Yeah, I can make this work, I think.

Sam's truck idled as he released a long sigh. He twisted in his seat and looked through the back window toward the bookstore. Elizabeth had dreamed of running this place, creating a certain kind of magic within these walls—something unspoken yet deeply felt. Now, watching Katie fight for those same dreams in her own way, Sam realized that maybe the best way to honor the past wasn't to hold onto it—but to find a way to build something new out of what was left.

9

Katie

Saturday

After spending weeks preparing for today, Katie stared at the plate of store-bought cookies, which she had rearranged for the thirteenth time. No matter how she shuffled them around, the plastic tray still screamed "last-minute effort."

Her phone read 9:58 a.m.—only two minutes before the Fall Book Festival officially started.

She had only set up thirty chairs, and even that felt stupidly optimistic. Laughable, even. The last few events had been brutal—mostly Emma and a handful of regulars who showed up, probably because they felt bad for her. At least she hadn't spent much on refreshments this time.

At exactly ten o'clock, the bell above the door chimed, and an elderly couple stepped inside. The wife paused to adjust her husband's scarf with a gentle tug before patting it into place.

Katie plastered on her best welcome smile, grateful that at least someone had shown up.

Then a mom hustled in with two kids, still wrestling with their jackets.

The bell chimed again ... and again.

Is this really happening?

Within an hour, the store was actually packed. Like, seriously packed. People were wedged between shelves, shoulder to shoulder, and every corner thrummed with vibrant conversations she hadn't heard in what felt like forever.

A heated debate about magical realism had broken out near the register, while Katie heard snippets of passionate recommendations floating from the young adult section: "You have to read this one," and "Just wait until you get to chapter three."

Katie's hands cramped as she rang up what felt like half the town, while simultaneously keeping an eye on the refreshment table. The snacks were disappearing faster than she could process payments.

And, naturally, today *would* be the day her dinosaur of a card reader decided to malfunction on every other swipe.

"Excuse me?" A woman stood on her toes, holding up a book from the biography section. "Do you carry this in hardcover?"

"Just a second!" Katie fumbled another credit card, painfully aware of the line now stretching all the way into the mystery aisles.

A quick glance behind the counter showed Benny sprawled out on his bed, snoring away like it was any other morning.

Must be nice.

A crash from the back of the store made her flinch, followed by a toddler's wail that rose like a siren from the picture book section.

The coffee maker made a sound that definitely meant trouble, and Katie felt her chest tighten.

This is too much. Way too—

The bell chimed again.

Katie nearly groaned—except she saw Sam step through the doorway.

He seemed to catch her panicked look and was already rolling up the sleeves of his flannel shirt, revealing muscular forearms with faint ink patterns that she didn't have time to be distracted by right now.

"Where do you need me?" His eyes scanned the room, and she could practically see him categorizing the chaos.

"Refreshments, register line, hardcover in children's, and—" Another crash echoed from the back, followed by several teenage voices saying "Oops" in unison. "That. Whatever *that* was."

Sam squeezed her shoulder as he passed, sending a spark down her arm that left her hyperaware of every nerve in her body. She watched as he navigated the chaos like a seasoned pro—restocking cookies, directing people to sections, and handling whatever disaster the teens had caused—all while she was still trying to convince the card reader that yes, it really did want to process payments today.

The bell chimed again, and a moment later Emma managed to circumvent the crowd and slip in next to Katie behind the cash register. "Whoa! When'd you become Insta-famous?"

"I didn't plan for this many people, and now everything's—" Katie gestured toward a kid scaling a shelf while his mom remained glued to her phone. Her gaze then darted to the refreshment table, and her stomach sank—it was completely empty. "We're out of everything."

"Say no more," Emma said, pulling out her keys. "Snack run it is."

"Please. Thank you. And maybe some juice? Oh, and coffee too!"

"On it." Emma disappeared into the sea of people as Sam returned.

"Finally found that hardcover for that lady," Sam said. "And the teens are handled. I convinced them rebuilding the display their way wasn't the best idea."

For a moment, she completely forgot about the chaos surrounding them.

"Thank you. I—" Katie touched his arm without thinking. At some point, he'd ditched the flannel for a fitted white T-shirt that clung to his broad shoulders. His messy hair gave him a disheveled charm that stirred—

"Hello? Some of us are waiting?" A man waved his book like a flag.

Focus, Katie. Focus.

The next few hours blurred into a kaleidoscope of faces as books changed hands, and the card reader beeped endlessly.

When the crowd finally thinned to something manageable, she found Sam had organized the *New Releases* table, the coffee maker had mysteriously started working again, and the teens had finally stopped stacking books into towers and recording themselves dancing around them—probably for TikTok. Even the card reader started behaving!

"You okay for now?" Sam asked.

Katie nodded. "Yeah, I've got it."

"Good. Here." He pulled a folded paper from his back pocket. "The checklist I worked on last night. Timeline's tight, but we can make it work."

Their fingers brushed as she took the paper, and neither pulled away immediately. The air seemed to shift between them, causing her stomach to flutter.

The pause lingered for a moment longer.

"I need to grab my tools from the truck and get started. Come find me if you need anything, okay?"

Anything?

Her mind immediately wandered where it—

Nope. Not going there.

She gave him a quick smile. "I will."

He nodded and headed toward the back door.

Katie tried not to stare, but come on—the way he moved in those jeans? She was only human.

The bell chimed and Emma walked in, loaded down with shopping bags. "The lines at the store were insane! But I come bearing snacks." She paused while setting out cookies, narrowing her eyes at Katie's face. "You okay?"

"I need to make an announcement."

"About?"

Katie took a breath, then another. "Everyone should know we might be closing. Don't want anyone surprised. But I just..."

"That feels a little early to say, but regardless of what happens, everything will work out. Okay?"

Katie began wringing her hands. "Do you think you could make the announcement? You're better with these types of things, you know? Public speaking. I don't want to say the wrong thing."

Emma grabbed her shoulders firmly as she looked Katie in the eye. "I love you, Katie. But this is your store. Your voice. You've got to be the one to say it."

Katie's throat felt like she'd swallowed sand.

"It's okay. I'll be here the whole time. You got this, girl."

Katie nodded as she cleared her throat. "Excuse me? ... Excuse me, can I have you, I-I mean everyone's attention, please?"

The remaining customers turned toward her.

A jolt of adrenaline coursed through her, making her knees feel as if they could buckle at any moment. Her fingers curled and uncurled at her sides, trying to find something solid to grasp. These weren't just random shoppers—they were neighbors, friends, and familiar faces.

"I need to tell you all something," she started with a shaky voice. "I'm not sure how to say this..." She paused as her gaze landed on the chalkboard near the register, where a crookedly written *Staff Picks* sign hung. "The city sent me a notice, which says I have a couple weeks to bring the building up to code, or they'll shut us down. And I'm not sure I'll be able to do everything that needs to be done to meet their deadline."

A ripple of whispers swept through the crowd.

"I tried that big bookstore in the city once, and they didn't even have a section for local authors. Where are we supposed to go if this place isn't here?" asked Mrs. Waters, holding onto her thriller novel.

"Remember Tommy's Harry Potter birthday?" someone called from the back. "Kid nearly took out a shelf with that wand, but you just laughed and gave him more cake."

"My daughter learned to read in that corner," a woman said from near the window. "She wouldn't read anywhere else."

"Town hall meeting's tomorrow afternoon," Old Pete said, shuffling forward. "We should all go. Let 'em know this ain't right."

A warmth spread through Katie as voices around her rose, sharing memories and offering support. She hadn't realized how deeply this place mattered to everyone, how many lives had been touched by her little bookstore off Main Street.

"Katie?" Ada's voice cut through the chatter like a knife.

She turned, expecting the woman's usual over-the-top cheeriness, but found her clutching her phone.

"Can I have a word?"

This can't be good.

Katie nodded and threaded her way through the bustle, following Ada into a quiet aisle near the back. "What's wrong?"

"It's about that handyman of yours." Ada practically shoved her phone under Katie's nose, forcing Katie to lean back to make sense of the image. "Knew I'd seen him before."

Katie's throat went dry as she stared at the photo of Sam who stood next to Derek in front of some fancy beach mansion on Hilton Head with the Huntington Properties logo behind them. Both were smiling, shaking hands. But it was the caption that made her lightheaded: *Another successful renovation with our top contractor.*

"Found it on The Facebook," Ada said gently. "It's from last year." She touched Katie's arm. "It could be nothing, but just in case … be careful, Katie. He could still be working for your ex, dear."

The renovation checklist in her pocket might as well have been a cinder block.

Katie's gaze drifted to the back room where Sam had disappeared. She thought about how seamlessly he'd blended into her world, like he'd always belonged there.

But had any of it been real?

Every smile, every touch, every moment they'd shared replayed in her mind.

Maybe she'd been naïve—again.

Just like she'd been with Derek.

What if Sam wasn't here to help?

What if this was part of Derek's plan—to send someone charming, someone who'd make her feel safe, only to pull the rug out from under her again?

The realization hit her like a punch to the gut.

How could she have let herself trust so quickly, and allowed these feelings—feelings she'd vowed never to let herself feel again?

10

Sam

Stepping out from the storage room, Sam adjusted his tool belt and watched the last few stragglers shuffle toward the door. He watched Katie with a customer, admiring how she lit up talking about books, how she remembered everyone's reading preferences, the way she created this safe space where stories mattered. She made everyone feel seen, special.

"Mom, come on!" A boy darted past, clutching a book to his chest. "I have to find out what happens to Harry!"

"Relax, Marcus, the book isn't going anywhere," his mom said, laughing as she followed.

Fingerprints smeared the windows, mysteries and romances piled together, and, somehow, a Stephen King hardcover sat wedged between plates of cookies at the refreshment table.

Katie stood at the register, sifting through a stack of receipts. The dark circles under her eyes should have made her look tired, but still, Sam found himself staring. Something in her posture seemed off.

"Hey." Sam stuffed a rag into his back pocket, catching Katie's glance. "Good news—the plumbing's all fixed. Wasn't too bad."

Katie nodded, still focused on her receipts.

"Oh, and the HVAC's done," he said, motioning toward the vents. "Just filters, a little duct cleaning, and tightening a few vents. Nothing major. I've got pictures if you want to see the before and after—"

"Are you working for Derek?"

The question knocked the air from his lungs.

Katie held up her phone. And there it was—that publicity photo from the beach house project. Him and Derek, shaking hands and smiling like they'd just solved world hunger instead of building some millionaire's summer getaway. His gut twisted at the memory of that day, not knowing what kind of man he was really working for at the time.

"No." Sam slid one hand into his pocket. "Not anymore."

Her eyes narrowed. "But you did?"

"Yeah," he admitted, rubbing the back of his neck with his other hand. "A few contracts here and there, over the years. One back home in Greenville. Another in Savannah. And Hilton Head." Sam rocked back on his heels. "There was this one here in Hadley Cove, but I didn't know what it was really about until yesterday. The second I figured it out, I quit."

"Why?"

"Because Derek's about to bulldoze half of Main Street. I can't be part of that.

And—"

"And?"

Sam met her eyes, and the truth just came out. "Because I met you." He pushed his hair back, knowing how it sounded but it needed to be said.

He watched the blush creep across her cheeks. "So, you're not trying to sabotage my business?"

"No, I'd never, but I think Derek might be." Sam paused and pulled out the crumpled inspection notice. "Look, something's really off with this letter. None of it adds up."

"And here I thought it was just me ..."

"It's not. Take that support beam in storage. Yeah, it's got water damage. And we'd need to dry everything out first, get some industrial fans and dehumidifiers in there. Then we'd have to take the weight off it, either reinforce or replace it, depending on how bad it is underneath. But it's fixable."

"And ..." She bit her bottom lip. "Sounds complicated."

"It's really not." He touched her arm without thinking. "You see, we'd put in temporary supports, and make sure everything's solid before we touch the damaged beam. Once that's fixed, we'd treat it so this doesn't happen again. Good as new."

"And we could get all of that done before the deadline?"

"That's the other thing." He tapped the notice. "For something like this, you'd usually get at least a month, sometimes two. But three weeks for a commercial building? That's ridiculous. I've done dozens of these projects, and I've never seen a timeline this tight."

A voice crackled from the small TV screen perched on the

counter. "Good afternoon, Hadley Cove." Mayor Williams stood at a podium with flags waving in the background. "Today, we're excited to share a bold vision for the future of our beloved town." She gestured to her left. "Here to explain the details is Derek Huntington, the lead developer for the project."

Sam and Katie exchanged a look.

"Hadley Cove deserves better," Derek said, sporting a polished smile with his suit and tie. "Our proposed development will create jobs, boost tourism, and revitalize the local economy. Together, we can transform this small town into the premier coastal destination."

The screen transitioned to a rendering. The familiar charm of Hadley Cove—the small businesses, the character, the history—was gone, replaced by something unrecognizable. Instead, there were gleaming hotels and upscale shops, and where Katie's bookstore should have been, a glass-fronted luxury boutique stretched toward the sky.

Sam's gaze flicked to Katie. Her lips parted slightly as though she'd forgotten to breathe.

Finally, she released a long sigh as her fingers moved in slow, aimless circles along the counter's edge. "There's a town hall tomorrow afternoon. I've never been to one, but it might be my only chance to ..."

"That's a great idea. But you don't seem so convinced. Why?" Sam asked.

"Well—" Katie fiddled with the already tidy stack of receipts, sliding each one into perfect alignment, over and over. "A few years ago, there was the wedding toast disaster—not mine, thankfully. Not that it would matter, now.

And before that, the first time I ever spoke in front of a crowd was my senior thesis presentation. Made it through exactly two sentences before my mind went completely blank. Just stood there, frozen, thirty pairs of eyes staring back at me. The professor had to escort me off the stage." She squared the corners of the papers again. "That was twenty years ago. You'd think I'd be over it by now, but ..."

"Doesn't matter if it's twenty years or twenty minutes—some things stick with you." Sam leaned on the counter, close enough to catch the faint scent of her shampoo.

"So how am I supposed to convince the whole town to save this place?"

"Look, Katie, I've seen you handle everything they've thrown at this store. You're more capable than you know."

She looked up at him. "You really think that?"

How can she not see it?

He reached for her hand, grasping it with his. "I do. You're wonderful, Katie."

She's more than wonderful—she's extraordinary.

When she squeezed his hand back, his thumb began brushing over her knuckles as if memorizing the moment. His pulse quickened, and he wondered if she could tell.

"I've been to a lot of town halls back home—mostly zoning meetings, but I know how they go, so I could help you prep, maybe practice what you want to say?"

Her smile widened and there was a sparkle in her eyes. "That would be amazing."

"You know I got you." Sam then looked around to survey the surrounding mess and reluctantly released her hand.

"But maybe we should clean this up first."

They quickly fell into a rhythm, working their way from fiction to non-fiction, biography to thriller, and then from fantasy to sci-fi.

Working side by side, he caught every detail: when her fingers glided over the book spines, pausing occasionally as if weighing whether each one belonged on the shelf or somewhere else entirely; how she'd smile at certain titles, as though they sparked a memory; or the way she'd stop to pick up a book and read a random passage aloud. Now and then, their hands would brush as they reached for the same book, and each time, Sam lost track of everything but the moment.

Later, when he'd asked why the children's section was organized by color, she had traced her fingers along the progression from red to violet and simply said, "Every kid deserves a rainbow."

That was Katie—always finding ways to make the world a little brighter.

There was a simple joy in the way she spoke that left him feeling both captivated and humbled. And that's when it hit him: He didn't just notice these things about her—he *felt* them. The warmth in her smile, her ability to breathe life into the smallest details, the effortless way she made him feel at home.

He felt it all.

They'd cleared most of the front section when Sam found a bookmark on the floor. He reached for it just as Katie did, and suddenly they were inches apart. The space between them felt impossibly small, and the air felt charged—like the moment before a summer storm. Katie's eyes lifted to his, and his pulse roared in his ears. For a second, the rest of the store disappeared.

He leaned in without thinking, and when she didn't pull away—

Woof! Woof!

Benny squeezed between them, tail going a mile a minute.

Katie stepped back, looking down with a soft laugh. "Someone needs his walk." She messed with her sleeve. "He doesn't let me forget his schedule."

"Well, don't mind me. Wouldn't want to keep y'all waiting." Sam's heart was still thrumming. "I could come back later? Help you get ready for tomorrow?"

"Sure, any help would be great." She gestured toward the snack table, still loaded with cookies that Emma had brought after most of the crowd had left. "Plus, there's enough sugar here to send someone into a coma. I'd rather not face that alone." She gave a light, self-deprecating chuckle.

"Great, it's a date," Sam said before realizing his mistake. His face burned. "I mean, uh—sounds like a plan. Seven work?"

This time when Katie smiled, it spread across her entire face. "Seven's perfect."

11

Katie

H 🗼 C

THE KEY JAMMED IN the lock, as usual: one wiggle left, two right, a firm push, and finally, a reluctant *click*.

When the door cracked open, Benny shouldered past Katie's legs with the distinct swagger of a dog who knew he'd gotten what he wanted. For someone who had snoozed through today's chaos, Benny had picked quite the moment to demand his walk—just as Sam had leaned in …

Way to go, Benny.

Benny bolted to his corner bed and collapsed, stretching out as if he'd run a marathon rather than their usual block loop.

"Drama queen," Katie muttered as she grabbed his water bowl. "*You* begged for the long walk, remember?"

Benny huffed a theatrical sigh and flopped onto his side, clearly unwilling to take any accountability.

She chuckled as she unzipped her jacket until—

Yep, stuck again.

Three tugs and an awkward, overhead shimmy later—she was free.

She hung up her jacket and flipped the sign to *Closed* fifteen minutes early—their Saturday wind-down ritual—and sank into the chair behind the table. Her Windows 7 laptop wheezed to life as she pulled up the day's numbers. The sales were good today. Surprisingly good. Maybe, just maybe, things were finally—

Then an email notification popped up in the screen's corner.

From: Raymond.Barnes@hadleycove.gov

Subject: Re: Building Inspection Notice

She clicked it faster than the notification could vanish.

Ms. Hayes,

All inspections are final. The violations listed must be corrected within the remaining nineteen days. This matter is not up for discussion.

Regards,

Raymond Barnes

Chief Building Inspector

And just like that, the bubble burst. She reached for her phone to call Sam, then froze—of course, they hadn't exchanged numbers yet.

Perfect. Just perfect.

Katie yanked open her desk drawer, pulling out index cards and markers. The town hall meeting was tomorrow at four. Sighing, she spread her supplies across the table; the scene looked like she was setting up for the world's most depressing art project.

Then again, the mere thought of standing in front of a

crowd, let alone giving a presentation, sent pins and needles skittering down her arms. But what choice did she have? She had to nail this presentation.

As she uncapped a black thin-point Sharpie, the familiar scent yanked her back to that night in the kitchen ...

Katie held the marker as she carefully outlined sections of a bookstore business plan on sheets of printer paper. After Derek had read her journal and mocked her bookstore dreams years ago, she'd done countless hours of research, determined to prove she could make it work.

"A bookstore?" Derek had barely glanced up from his phone and laughed. "We're back to this fantasy again?"

She'd tried to explain, pointing at the numbers and notes she'd painstakingly written out. "It's different now. I've created actual projections. Look at the numbers ... See? It could work. I only need—"

"What?" He cut her off with a smirk. "You need me to fund your little hobby? First it was scribbling dreams in your diary, now you're playing entrepreneur with printer paper? No offense, but you haven't really accomplished much in the professional world. And you think you can run a business? Now, that's funny."

His words stung worse than a slap. "Just forget it, Derek. Sorry I brought it up."

He always had a way of making her feel about two inches tall. By bedtime, she'd nearly convinced herself he was right. Maybe she wasn't cut out for any of this.

Katie tossed the Sharpie down, watching it roll across the table until it hit her laptop. She snatched the computer, pulled it onto her lap, and before she could stop herself she was typing *Huntington Properties* into Facebook. Her finger hovered over the trackpad as results populated the screen.

Corporate announcements, job listings, customer complaints ... She scrolled past them all, her heart beating a little faster with each flick of her wrist.

There it was—the photo Ada had shown her—of Derek and Sam in front of some mega-beach mansion, doing that fake handshake thing people do in business photos. Last year—according to the timestamp.

She clicked on the tagged name: *Sam Everett.*

When the profile loaded, his smile in the small picture was unmistakable—confident, maybe even a little smug. The kind of smile that said he knew exactly what he was doing.

Then she saw it: *Married to Elizabeth Everett.*

Wait, what?

Her heart dropped into her shoes.

He's—? But we almost— When he—

Her fingers had a mind of their own, or at least what she told herself as she clicked Elizabeth's name.

The profile picture loaded: Sam and Elizabeth—at the Wishing Tree Festival two years ago. Then came the caption: *Another perfect night.*

Katie pressed her palm against her chest. She closed out

of the profile picture, scrolled further, and—

"Oh ... Oh no."

Memorial posts filled the page. Dozens of them. Her eyes skipped from one to the next, each one more gut-wrenching than the last.

Rest in peace.

Gone too soon.

We'll miss you so much.

A GoFundMe link: *Help Sam cover his late wife's funeral costs and medical bills.*

The amount raised was painful to look at. Barely enough to cover basics.

When Katie clicked the link, the comments section pulled her in like quicksand.

Elizabeth was so excited to show me the new shelves Sam built for the children's corner. Can't believe she never got to see them filled with books. Miss you so much, sweet friend.

Her hand shook as she kept scrolling.

Sam, no one should have to choose between more time and keeping their dream alive. Selling the store was the right choice. Elizabeth knew that. Praying for you.

The words dissolved into a haze as her vision blurred with tears.

Remember when you told me your grandmother's bookstore was what made you fall in love with reading? You were going to give that gift to so many other kids. Life is so unfair sometimes.

Her scrolling froze mid-flick.

There, below the comment, was a photo that made her whole body go cold.

A little girl sitting on an old lady's lap—the exact photo

from her storage room that Sam had stared at.

Wait...

Katie's knees wobbled as she went to stand. The room felt too warm, too small. But still, she forced herself forward and moved to the lockbox behind the register.

Opening it, her trembling hands sifted through old receipts and Christmas cards from regulars until she unearthed the store's deed, buried at the very bottom. Her eyes scanned the document, past Summit Valley Realty's notary stamp and transfer details. Then her gaze landed on the previous owners' signatures.

Elizabeth Everett and Sam Everett

301 Ivy Lane

Greenville, SC 29601

The room tilted sideways as blood rushed from Katie's head.

The deed slipped through her fingers, and she grabbed the edge of the table, willing the nausea to pass.

This had been *their* store. *Their* dream. *Elizabeth's* dream.

Everything fell into place with awful clarity—horribly painful clarity.

That wish Sam had been looking for that first night... the way he'd touched each ribbon, read every tag like his life depended on it... how he'd touched that old photograph like it was made of glass.

Katie couldn't even be mad that Sam hadn't told her. She just felt sad—for him, for Elizabeth, for all their dreams that had died before Elizabeth had ever gotten a chance to run this place.

Yet through it all, here was Sam, fighting to save the store he'd once been forced to let go of—a piece of Elizabeth he'd had to give up—just so Katie wouldn't have to lose her own dream the way he'd lost his.

In that moment, as Benny's soft snores filled the silence, Katie let her tears fall freely for every heartbeat of love and loss these walls had absorbed before she'd ever turned the key.

12

Sam

THE DOOR CHIMED AS Sam stepped into Miller's Hardware, ducking his head beneath the low doorframe. The place smelled like his grandfather's workshop—a mix of sawdust and metal. A heater clicked somewhere in the back, though it did little to chase away the chill, and a Buddy Holly tune crackled through the static on an old radio. The big box stores might be prettier, but good luck finding someone who knew which screw could actually hold a shelf up.

His boots squeaked against the linoleum as he grabbed a wire basket, mentally ticking off the list for Katie's repairs: screws, adhesive, painter's tape … nothing fancy. Just the basics.

The aisles were narrow, crammed with everything from pipe fittings to picture hangers. Paint brushes shared shelf space with spark plugs. Somehow a garden hose had ended up next to a box of doorknobs, which nobody had moved since '82, if the layer of dust was anything to go by. Organization wasn't exactly the priority here—this was decades of "it's always been there" logic. Still, he managed to collect everything he needed.

At the register, an older woman worked on a crossword puzzle, ash-white hair pulled back in a no-nonsense bun and reading glasses dangling from a tarnished chain that had probably seen every sale since the Carter administration. Her name tag—slightly tilted—

read, *Ruth*.

"Find everything okay?" Ruth asked, without looking up. Her voice carried the tone of someone who had seen too many long days and too few easy ones.

Sam set his basket down at the counter. "Yes, ma'am."

A door creaked behind the register, and a man in paint-splattered coveralls appeared, carrying a stack of papers. His name tag read, *George*.

"Any luck?" Ruth's voice had an edge to it.

"Left another message." George dropped the papers with a sigh. "For all the good it'll do."

The scanner beeped three times before Ruth's shaking fingers managed to line up a single barcode.

"Got our notice yesterday," she said, looking at Sam. "Twenty-one days to fix everything, or that's it for us."

Sam's hand froze halfway to his wallet.

Twenty-one days?

Ruth gestured around the store. "Half this stuff wasn't even flagged on our last inspection."

"You could say this place is as old as that Philco there." George nodded toward the radio. "And it's seen more years than half our customers. Still works most days, too."

"That's right, November '56. My daddy just got back from Korea when he decided to open this place." Ruth smiled. "I was just a kid, sorting bolts while everyone raved about Elvis's movie playing at the Strand—*Love Me Tender*." She shook her head. "Whole town turned out for that one."

Sam's jaw clenched as the pieces clicked into place—*Derek*.

"We'll be at town hall tomorrow." George squeezed Ruth's shoulder. "Not that it matters. Mayor Williams sold this town out to that developer months ago."

Sam wanted to help. Really. But he was already committed to Katie's repairs. Plus, his bank account was running off fumes.

"That'll be thirty-two sixteen," Ruth said.

Sam handed over two twenties. "Keep the change."

"Oh, we couldn't—"

"Please, put it toward the repairs."

Ruth's eyes welled up as she bagged his stuff.

To Sam, kindness had always been a strange sort of currency—easy to give, harder to accept, and yet it always seemed to come when it was needed most.

"See you at town hall?" George called out as Sam reached the door.

Sam hesitated before answering. "Yeah. I'll be there."

Back at the Sandy Shores Inn, Sam caught his reflection in the mirror and couldn't help but feel ridiculous. The warm glow from the bedside lamp wasn't doing much to help—if anything, it made the whole room feel weirdly intimate, as if he were preparing for a high school movie date—like the one where his mom had to drop him off and pick him up because he didn't have a license.

Sam had changed shirts twice already, the rejects tossed onto the bed where they would probably stay wrinkled until morning. He ended up deciding on a white T-shirt, while his least wrinkled flannel hung on the bathroom door. He kept glancing at it, knowing he'd probably end up wearing it anyway.

After slipping on dark jeans, he put on a pair of socks and his work boots. The old pleather boots were still dark in patches from his attempt to clean them with the inn's towel, but at least he had knocked most of the dust off them. Besides, they had walked him through plenty of jobs and long days—might as well see him through tonight, too.

Sam ran a hand through his hair, giving up on the salt-and-pepper mess. Elizabeth used to crack up about his permanent bedhead—said he looked like he had just rolled out of a trendy coffee shop's Instagram feed.

The body spray sat on the dresser where he had unpacked it yesterday—a Secret Santa gift from Elizabeth's grandmother, years ago. Barely used it. In fact, he only wore it on—

But this isn't a date ... right?

He shook his head and grabbed the canister. The pine scent hit him as he sprayed it, and suddenly he was in their Greenville kitchen ...

Elizabeth spun around in mismatched socks, half-singing, half-humming, while she slapped together a peanut butter sandwich with a side of whatever was left in the fridge.

"You smell like a broke contractor who's three Smirnoff Ice's deep at O'Malley's on karaoke night," she had said, scrunching her nose as she handed him the plate.

"Yeah, well, you married this broke contractor."

"And I've loved every moment of us."

"Me too ..."

Sam blinked away the memory.

A bittersweet ache settled in his chest—still, he managed a small smile. In another life, Elizabeth and Katie would've been friends.

The thought stopped his breath mid-inhale. It shouldn't have been comforting, but somehow, it was.

Sam shook his head. Some thoughts weren't worth chasing tonight. Tonight was about helping Katie get ready for the town hall.

Not a date.

Sam gave himself a final once-over in the bathroom mirror, adjusting his shirt like it would make a difference before he threw on his flannel.

His phone buzzed near the sink. With a quick downward glance, he noted the alarm he had set earlier now lit up the screen: 6:45 p.m. He shut it off and grabbed his keys.

Time to go.

13

Katie

How do I tell him?

The streetlamp traced the silver in Sam's hair as he approached the store. Katie's hand paused on the door handle, and she watched him through the glass, trying to ignore how her stomach fluttered at the sight of him.

She knew she should tell Sam—about finding Elizabeth's photos, about how she'd pieced together that this used to be their store. But how would she even begin that conversation?

Hey, sorry your wife died, and you had to sell her dream store to pay for her medical bills, but thanks for helping me keep it going? ... Ugh.

Maybe it would be best to wait for him to bring it up, if he ever did.

She pulled the door open, and Sam stepped inside.

He looked good. Unfairly good for someone in just a flannel over a white T-shirt and dark jeans. Even his boots looked cleaner, and though his hair still seemed messy—this time it appeared purposefully so. Not that she was noticing these things. Except she totally was.

Benny scrambled over to Sam, nearly toppling over the stack of books by the door.

"Benny, don't be so clingy," Katie said, tugging gently at his collar.

"He's just being a good boy. It's fine, really." Sam took a knee, ruffling the dog's wiry hair. He grinned as his eyes met Katie's. "Long time no see."

Katie smirked. "Hey stranger."

"So, how are you?" The playfulness in his voice shifted to something gentler.

"Good, everything's good." The words felt fake. She had gotten pretty skilled at that lately—saying she was fine when everything was falling apart.

"Sounds convincing." Sam stood up, catching her eye. Something in his face made her want to look away, but she couldn't. "But here's the thing ... When I ask, 'How are you?' I always want the real version. Every word—all of it."

The tenderness in his voice cracked something open inside her. "The inspector got back to me. E-mailed. Said the inspection is final." The words still stung, even after reading them twenty times.

Sam's arms moved around her. He was solid and warm, and he smelled like pine mixed with citrus and sandalwood.

"We're gonna figure this out ... together." His voice rumbled through his chest where her cheek rested on it.

Together ...

Katie held on a little longer than she probably should have before stepping back. "This way."

She led him to the cozy corner couch and coffee table where she had set up snacks, drinks, her pile of index cards, and markers. The sight reminded her of those early days in the store, when she had brought in homemade snacks for events and people had actually shown up.

Sam dropped onto the couch; the cushions sank under his weight, bringing the two of them closer together. He began checking out the spread. "Looks perfect, though you didn't have to go through all the trouble."

Me go through ALL the trouble? After ALL you've done here—for this place, for me, for Elizabeth?

"Heh. No worries. It wasn't any trouble at all."

A snout peeked at the edge of the table as Benny made his move for the good stuff.

Katie pointed her finger at him. "No, no, Benny!" She nodded toward his fancy orthopedic bed in the corner, one of many scattered around the bookstore and the apartment.

Benny groaned like she'd ruined his whole life, then dragged himself to his bed and flopped down.

He should be more grateful.

She turned and saw Sam reach for one of her homemade fried pickles, trying not to care too much about what he thought. Should she have made something different?

Sam took a bite and his eyes widened. "Okay. This ... this is in-CRED-ible."

"The air fryer is seriously the best appliance ever invented."

"Can't argue with that."

Katie let out the breath she was holding. "They're vegan, too. I noticed you ordered the Beyond burger at Phil's."

"Oh man, I didn't even think about the breading—usually has milk in it. Been vegan since last month, actually. Still figuring out what I can and can't eat." He grabbed another pickle. "Not many people would go out of their way like this."

She smiled. "Not many people would offer to help save someone else's store."

They both chuckled, and he took another bite, chewing thoughtfully. "Thanks for putting all this together. Very unexpected. Can't remember the last time I had something home cooked for me."

"Well, home air-fried ..."

"Still counts. Appreciate you a ton."

"Thanks." She grinned as he grabbed another.

It was such a simple thing—fried pickles in the air fryer—but how Sam lit up, you'd think she'd spent all day in the kitchen.

With Derek, it had always been "What's for dinner?" the moment he walked through the door, like she was some sort of vending machine that dispensed meals on demand. Even her elaborate Sunday brunches had been met with nothing more than a grunt and maybe a "needs more salt" suggestion.

Eventually she had stopped hoping for even a passing compliment.

The way Sam smiled, the way he appreciated something so small, said more than words ever could—it wasn't just about the food. It was about being seen. And for the first

SINCE THE DAY WE WISHED 99

time in what felt like forever, Katie started to believe that maybe she was exactly what

someone needed ...

—ele—

From the couch, Katie pushed the plates of snacks toward the edge of the coffee table, making room to spread out her note cards. Despite having rewritten them three times, she cringed at her messy handwriting. They still looked like a third grader's book report.

"I don't even know where to start. I've written down some random thoughts, but ..." She stared at the words until they stopped making sense.

"Well, you have to start somewhere. That's the hardest part. And you've done that." Sam leaned forward, his knee brushing hers.

Little sparks shot up her leg at the contact.

"You know," he continued, "at the town halls I've been to, the people who got through to the council—who got things changed—were the ones who spoke from the heart."

Katie's hand went to her chin. "Makes sense."

"Yeah, they made it personal, but also tied it to the bigger picture. Maybe we should start there—connect how the store means so much to you with how it serves the community and the people who love it."

"Sounds doable."

Sam picked up one of her cards, turning it to face her. "Like this one about the kids' reading program—it's perfect. It shows what the store means to you personally, but also how it impacts local families."

Their fingers grazed as he handed her the card, sending a jolt passing through her.

She grabbed another card. "And what about the senior book club? Mrs. Waters told me last week it was the highlight of her month. Some of them have been meeting here for years."

"Exactly." Sam nodded, leaning in to read her notes. His shoulder pressed against hers as he sorted through different cards. "And here—the local author showcases. You're giving people in town a platform they wouldn't have otherwise. See? It all starts flowing when you just let yourself talk about what matters."

Now and then, their hands would meet as they reached for the same card. But what struck Katie most was how Sam truly listened—like her ideas mattered. He wasn't just helping her organize words on cards. He was helping her believe she *could* do this.

But when Katie reached for a cookie, she froze as Derek's voice popped into her head.

Should you really be eating that? You've already had two.

Then all those digs came rushing back—Derek watching what she ate, making comments about her clothes, judging *every* little thing. She had spent too many years trying to make herself smaller, quieter, less ... But now, years later, his voice still crept in sometimes, making her second-guess everything.

Still, she picked up the cookie, except—Sam was now watching her.

"What? Do I have something on my face?"

"No." His voice went quiet. "I just ... I don't want to look away."

Katie's breath caught, and as she released it, a nervous laugh surfaced. She brushed a stray lock of hair behind her ear. "You know, you're dangerous with lines like that."

Sam grinned, leaning closer. "It's not a line if it's true."

Katie picked up a notecard, then set it down again. "I should probably mention the community events in my speech."

"Like those costume parties in the photos?" Sam asked.

"Exactly." She tucked a strand of hair behind her ear. "The Pride and Prejudice tea party was my favorite. Everyone went all out with the costumes." She smiled at the memory. "Mr. Clark from the bakery complained about his cravat the entire time, though I caught him practicing his bow in the window reflection."

"Let me guess—you were Elizabeth Bennet?"

"Actually, no. The costume shop mixed up my order." She laughed. "But it worked out. Elizabeth's great, but there's something about Mr. Darcy ..." She felt her cheeks flush. "Should probably focus on the speech though. Can't exactly save the store by gushing about Mr. Darcy all night."

"Right?" Sam smiled.

As the next hour flew by, she began to feel more confident about tomorrow. Together, they had crafted solid points about the store's impact on the community and how it gave people a place to belong.

Katie gathered the note cards, stacking them neatly to

bring as backup for tomorrow.

"This is honestly the sweetest thing anyone's done for me in ... well, forever." She looked at Sam.

"My pleasure. I had fun being with you."

"And I know you mean it. It's crazy." "What is?" "That someone actually believes in me. After, you know, Derek ..."

"Not every guy out there is like Derek." Sam's hand covered hers where it rested on her knee. "What happened between you two, anyway? Besides him being a massive jerk."

Katie's fingers twitched beneath his and she found herself staring at their hands—how his fingers curled around hers. It felt so natural. "I got tired of never feeling like enough. Ultimately, I decided being alone was better than being walked on. I should've listened to my parents—they never liked him."

"Of course, he begged me to take him back, but I wouldn't. Since then, he's done little things to intimidate me: texts, spreading rumors, showing up here and just watching me. Those kinds of things. Thought about reporting it, but who would ever believe me? He's this hotshot developer and I'm just ... no one. So, I just try to keep to myself."

Sam's hand found hers again, squeezing gently. It pulled her back from those dark memories. "I believe you. And, Katie?"

She looked at him.

His eyes locked onto hers. "You're more than enough. You always have been."

Sam's words unraveled something deep within her,

something she hadn't realized she'd been holding onto—that sometimes it takes someone else to remind you of what you've forgotten about yourself. Katie could feel how deeply he cared. Not only with the things he said or all the big things he had done for her since they had met, but in smaller ways—how he looked at her like he was seeing her for the first time, again and again.

The space between them on the couch seemed to vanish without either of them moving, but Sam was leaning in, and this time there were no customers around, no Benny interrupting, no reason to stop. It was so easy to lean in as well, to meet him halfway.

Then, before she could think twice, they kissed.

His lips pressed against hers, sparking a thousand tingles through her nerves. As the rush subsided, Katie managed to relax. They fit like two puzzle pieces into each other's worlds, creating something wholly their own—just him, just her, just this. Everything else disappeared—the store's problems, tomorrow's presentation, even the guilt about Elizabeth. And then—

Woof! Woof!

They broke apart to find Benny looking way too pleased with himself as he sat there with his leash in his mouth.

Katie laughed, running her fingers through her hair as her face burned. "Better timing tonight, boy."

Sam laughed too and stood up slowly, though his hand lingered on her shoulder. "I should let you take him out. You need to rest up for tomorrow, anyway."

Who needs rest? "Yeah, I probably should."

"Want me to pick you up tomorrow? We could ride to the

town hall together. Say around a quarter to four?"

Katie nodded, her lips still buzzing. "I'll be ready."

Sam pulled her into a hug before leaving, and Katie let herself sink into it, breathing in that mix of pine and citrus one more time. His arms tightened around her, like maybe he wasn't ready to let go either. When they finally parted, his eyes held that same warmth from earlier.

As Katie watched him go, a long sigh escaped her.

Maybe people do come into your life at exactly the right moment.

14

Sam

Though his truck waited in the lot, his feet carried him in the opposite direction. Heading back to the inn wasn't an option—not with his jumbled thoughts. Between helping Katie with tomorrow's town hall speech and that moment on the couch, his head was spinning.

He knew where he needed to go.

Where he'd first met Elizabeth.

Where he'd made his last promise to her.

The place he'd been avoiding for two years.

The Wishing Tree.

The gravel path crunched under his boots, while the faint aroma of fried dough and roasted peanuts hung in the air from the darkened vendor stalls and empty food trucks. Despite it being the last night of the festival, Main Street was quieter than he had expected.

As he neared the Wishing Tree, the quiet deepened. Most of the crowd had cleared out, leaving overflowing trash bins and empty cups strewn across the ground for the morning crew to deal with. A few stragglers lingered: a couple strolling arm in arm, a teenager stretched on his tiptoes, tying one last ribbon before turning away—and an older man sitting alone on a bench, who looked to have the weight of the world on his shoulders. Sam caught his eye, and they exchanged quick nods before he turned his attention to the tree.

Sam took a step forward and inhaled.

Maybe tonight he would finally find Elizabeth's purple ribbon.

His hands moved slowly as he began combing through the lower branches. Each glimpse of purple sent his heart racing. He lifted the first one his eyes spotted, reading the neat block letters of the wish: *Happiness for my family.* Swallowing the lump in his throat, Sam carefully returned it. Not hers.

Further down, another flash of purple. This one made his breath hitch—until he saw the message was in Spanish. His shoulders sagged.

At this rate, he could be here all night.

He glanced at his phone—eleven o'clock. His fingertips were starting to go numb from the cold, but he couldn't stop now. Not when he might be this close.

Another purple ribbon, then another—wrong shades, wrong handwriting. His searching grew frantic until something grabbed his attention, tucked behind a cluster of red and blue ribbons. He slowed down and moved the other ribbons aside.

There it was—the perfect shade of purple.

Is this—

He grasped it in his palm and turned it over.

The handwriting leaped out at him, unmistakable in its slanted loops and neat curves, like the sticky notes she'd used to leave everywhere: *Don't forget bread* on his steering wheel, *Love you* on his wallet, and *You've got this* on his toolbox before big jobs. This was Elizabeth's ribbon!

His heart hammered against his ribs.

The tag's wrapping crinkled as her words came into focus.

Sam,
I wish that someday you'll learn to love
and to be loved again.
Forever yours,
Elizabeth.

Even in the end, she'd thought of his future—of what they'd lost and all she hoped he might find again. That was Elizabeth—always taking care of everyone else.

Sam tried to hold himself together—he really did—but the tears came anyway, followed by a quiet sob. Over the years, he'd come to understand that tears weren't always about sadness; sometimes, they were simply proof that a heart was still trying to heal.

Sam flinched as a hand rested on his shoulder.

"You okay, son?" It was the old man from the bench.

Sam swiped his sleeve across his face, though he probably wasn't fooling anyone. "Yeah, I'm good." His voice came out rough. "Just, uh, tears of joy. Sort of."

The old man's face softened like he got it. "Glad to hear it."

Sam cleared his throat. "Thanks. So, what's got you out here this late?"

A knowing smile tugged at the corners of the old man's mouth. "Could ask you the same thing."

They both chuckled, and some of the heaviness lifted. Sam was grateful for the moment to pull himself together.

"Did you make a wish tonight?" Sam asked, nodding at the tree.

"Nah, made mine years ago." The man pointed to the ground. "It's one of these flowers now."

Sam looked at the wildflowers surrounding the tree's base. He had walked past them without a second thought. "What do you mean?"

"Oh, you must be new in town."

"Sort of. It's ... complicated."

"Everything in life is, ain't it?" The old man bent down and touched a flower. "These wishes work different here. They're special."

"How's that?"

"See, the paper's got seeds in it. You write your wish and you wrap it up in this stuff to protect the tag—kind of like cellophane, but it breaks down over time. Natural-like."

Sam lifted a newer wish, turning it over. The way the lights caught the cellophane reminded him of his windows at home when it rained. "What about the ribbons? They seem sturdy."

"Tencel. Breaks down too. You write your name on it, tie it all together." He motioned to the branches. "Hang it up, then let nature do its thing. Rain gets to the cellophane first. Then the paper starts going. But those seeds?" The old man grinned. "They're just waiting. Before you know it, flowers are popping up everywhere. Some like the shade under the tree, others stretch out to the sunny spots. Each one finds its place. Nothing goes to waste here."

Sam lowered himself to one knee. His fingers hovered over a white petal before touching it with the same care he had used with the ribbons. The flowers shimmered under the moonlight, scattered across the ground like tiny stars. Each had started as a wish, transforming into something entirely new, yet no less beautiful. Like how his grief had grown into something else—not replacing what he'd lost but existing alongside it.

"Do you believe wishes come true?" Sam asked.

"Yeah, I do." The man's gaze drifted up through the branches. "Seen some miracles happen from this tree with my own eyes. Actually, came to make a new one tonight. Might wait, though—got some things to fix first." He kicked at the dirt. "I made some bad calls lately. Hurt people I never meant to. Didn't want to, but felt backed into a corner, you know?"

Sam rose and dusted off his jeans. "Sounds like a pretty difficult situation."

"You ain't lying. I could make it right though, but ..." He shook his head. "Might lose everything if I do."

Sam reflected on his decision to walk away from Derek's project—and the growing stack of bills back home. "We'll never regret doing the right thing," he said. "No matter how hard it is. We can always begin again."

"Begin again ..." The old man rolled the words around, like he was testing them. After a minute, he looked at Sam differently, like he was seeing someone else. "You remind me of my boy. Lost him a few years back."

"I'm sorry to hear that." Sam knew how hollow those words could sound, but sometimes they were all you had.

The old man nodded and checked his watch. "I should head home. Cat's probably wondering where dinner is." He began to leave, but turned back. "Say, what's your name, son?"

Sam stuck out his hand. "Sam. Good to meet you, sir."

"Raymond." His handshake was firm. "Nice meeting you, young man."

15

Katie

Sunday

WHAT IF I MESS up? What if Derek's there?

The questions tumbled through Katie's mind on repeat as Sam's truck rolled into the town hall parking lot. The red brick building had always stood as a symbol of small-town democracy. Today, it felt more like an arena.

Her hands trembled as she shuffled the index cards, trying to steady herself.

"You're gonna crush it." Sam reached over and squeezed her hand, as if he could read her mind.

"Easy for you to say." She'd been up half the night practicing in front of her bathroom mirror until Benny had started howling along. Not to mention, she hadn't even managed to eat breakfast—unless you counted the half a granola bar Benny had guilted her into sharing during their morning walk.

Sam turned off the engine, and there it was—Derek's black Tesla, claiming the spot right by the entrance. Front and center, just like always.

They stepped out of the truck and rushed past a crookedly taped *No Food or Beverages Allowed* sign on the double doors. Inside, the place was already packed. They found seats in the back row, which was fine by Katie—smaller chance of being spotted by Derek. The plastic folding chairs squeaked on the tile under the weight of what had to be half the town.

She recognized most of the faces. Old Pete gave her a little wave from his seat a few rows up. Ruth and George from Miller's Hardware had shown up, sharing what looked like a contraband bag of chips between them. A group of teens huddled near the water fountain—probably the same ones that had turned her historical fiction section into a Jenga tournament yesterday. They kept checking their phones and whispering, likely debating whether to record the outcome of today's town hall disaster or not—but at least they'd shown up.

Katie's gaze moved to the center table where the council members and mayor sat. Mayor Williams was tapping away at her phone like she had better places to be. Her blazer and lipstick shared the same shade of power red—no way was that a coincidence. She looked exactly like she had when Katie first moved here over ten years ago: not a strand of dyed black hair out of place, pearl earrings, and that same air of polished authority that made even grocery store runs feel like campaign events. The woman hadn't changed, right down to how she glanced at her watch every few minutes as if counting down the seconds until she could leave.

"You okay?" Sam nudged Katie's arm.

"Not really." She picked at a loose thread on her sleeve. "Last time I had to speak in front of Derek, I completely froze. It was at our friends' wedding—I had this toast all planned, but..." She shook her head. "Let's just say I haven't been asked to make another one since."

Sam laced his fingers through hers. "That was then. This is now."

Before Katie could respond, Mayor Williams tapped her microphone, making everyone wince. "Good afternoon, everyone. As you know, there's been concern about the Hadley Cove development project. So, I'd like to welcome Derek Huntington, who will address these issues."

Katie's throat went dry as Derek approached the podium. His tailored suit fit like it had been measured to the millimeter, and his dark brown hair was slicked back with the same maddening precision that she remembered all too well. And then there was that smug smile—the one that used to make her feel so small—along with the blue tie she had given him for their tenth anniversary. She couldn't decide if the sight of it made her want to throw up or laugh.

"Change is inevitable," Derek started. "This development will bring jobs, tourism, and a fresh start for Hadley Cove. Our projections show a sixty percent city revenue growth in the first year alone. Therefore, the old ideas of what this town ought to be must make way for the new..."

Chairs scraped against the tile as people leaned forward,

exchanged glances, crossed and uncrossed their arms. Fragments of whispered conversations floated around Katie.

"Rent's going up. It's just a matter of time," the woman next to Sam muttered to her husband. "We can barely afford it now. Where are we supposed to go?"

"My grandmother's lived in that house for forty years," someone hissed from two rows away. "They can't just tear it down."

Ada's floral perfume drifted over as she leaned forward. "The nerve of that man, showing his face after what he's doing to our town."

One by one, local business owners took their turns at the podium. Mr. Clark of Sweet Dreams Bakery talked about his grandfather starting with only fifty dollars and a dream. Mrs. White of Harbor Blooms, who always gave Katie extra flowers for her window display, worried about competing with some fancy garden center. Then there was Mrs. Steinfeld of The Daily Grind, who saved Katie's sanity with free coffee during a power outage, jabbing her finger at the council as she listed off every wedding proposal, graduation celebration, and wake that her shop had hosted since 1973.

Derek had an answer for everything, twisting their words until they sounded "selfish and short-sighted," "too focused on the past," and "not seeing the bigger picture." The council nodded along, clearly already sold on his vision of progress.

"Think of the tourism potential," Derek said for what felt like the hundredth time. "The revenue stream. The opportunities. Change can be difficult, but—"

"And what about *our* jobs?" someone called out. "Our homes?"

Derek's smile didn't waver. "I understand change is unsettling, but sometimes we have to think bigger than our personal comfort. For the greater good."

Katie's heart sank as she watched speaker after speaker fail to make a dent. Charlie Callahan, owner of Sole Revival, who'd fixed her boots last winter, couldn't even finish his speech after having an on-stage breakdown. Mrs. Sanders, from Threadworks Boutique, tried explaining how three generations of her family had built their business, but Derek just talked over her about "fixed mindsets" versus "growth mindsets."

"Final call for comments," Mayor Williams announced, checking her watch again.

The room went quiet except for someone's baby fussing in the back.

It's now or never.

Katie's pulse pounded in her ears, drowning out everything else.

Sam moved a hand to her knee. "You got this."

Her legs felt like jelly as she rose. "I'd like to speak."

—ele—

The podium might as well have been on the other side of town.

Are people staring?

On the walk down the center aisle, Katie focused on

counting floor tiles to keep her mind occupied, and tried not to look at anyone directly, especially Derek. As she arrived, her heel caught on the steps up to the stage and she stumbled.

Someone snickered—probably one of the council members.

When she finally stepped onto the stage, the bright, unflattering lights illuminated every corner, leaving nowhere to hide. She might as well have been under interrogation.

At the podium, she reached for her index cards. But her pocket was empty.

Oh, no. The cards. In Sam's truck.

She froze, and her mind went completely blank.

The silence dragged on.

Someone coughed ...

The AC sputtered and clanked overhead ...

This was exactly what had happened at that wedding—standing there like an idiot while everyone stared. Derek's voice replayed in her head: *Maybe next time you'll think twice before volunteering for something you can't handle. You're not exactly a natural at this.*

Her breath grew shallow as she clutched the podium, eyes scanning the room, searching for something—someone—anyone who could help. Her eyes darted to the back row where Sam had been sitting earlier.

His seat was empty.

Of course, he stepped out.

Then the doors at the back flew open, pulling her attention.

Katie's jaw dropped as her regulars poured in. Old

Pete led the charge dressed as Gandalf, complete with a staff and beard. Behind him, Mrs. Waters strolled in, fully Mary Poppins, umbrella and all. The Martinez family came next—Mr. and Mrs. Martinez, with their three kids all dressed as the Pevensie children from Narnia, with little Rosa proudly wearing a toy bow like Susan. Katie's best friend Emma brought up the rear, dressed as Hermione Granger, with her rescue dog Riley sporting a perfect Padfoot costume, complete with shaggy black fur and a doggy Azkaban collar.

Then Sam appeared, and Katie almost forgot how to breathe. He was full-on Mr. Darcy, right down to the cravat. That one piece of hair still fell across his forehead, though, and somehow that made it perfect.

They carried signs made from her old promotional posters: "Stories Matter Here." "Save Breezy Tails!" "Our Town, Our Stories, Our Choice!" Someone had even strung together tiny origami books like a paper chain.

"You got this, Katie!" Old Pete bellowed, cupping his hands around his mouth.

Something shifted inside her. These people—her people—they got it. They understood what her store meant to this town. What stories could do. What community really meant.

She planted her palms against the podium, straightened her shoulders, and started speaking straight from the heart.

"Hadley Cove isn't just another small town. It's a community built on stories—your stories." Her voice got stronger with each word. "Every day I watch kids discover new worlds between pages. I see teenagers find characters who make them feel less alone. I hear grandparents sharing their favorite books with their grandkids."

She turned to face the council. "Progress shouldn't erase what makes us special—it should build on what already works. It should build bridges, not burn them. My store might not be perfect, but it's home for the people who need one. A place where stories connect us. Where everyone belongs."

Derek stepped forward. "It's simple economics. Small businesses like yours can't compete—"

The crowd drowned him out with cheers and chants. "Save our stores!" Mr. Martinez's wooden shield nearly knocked over a standing lamp and Old Pete's staff got tangled in Mrs. Waters' umbrella, but they kept cheering anyway.

Mayor William's voice rang out over the speakers. "Ladies and gentlemen, let me remind you that this is a discussion about the future of Hadley Cove—a future we all have a stake in. Let's ensure we keep this respectful." Her attention then moved to Katie. "Thank you, Ms. Hayes. You may take your seat."

Katie's legs wobbled as she stepped down from the podium, but she lifted her chin. She had done it. She had stood up there, faced Derek, and spoken her truth. The crowd's applause hadn't just been for the speech—it had been for her.

She glanced back toward the podium, catching Derek's slumped shoulders, and couldn't stop the small, satisfied smile that crept onto her face.

When she arrived at her seat, Sam was already standing. He wrapped an arm around her, pulling her close. She leaned into him, breathing in that mix of pine and citrus she was starting to associate with good things. The best things.

Mayor Williams tapped the microphone again. "The council will take a fifteen-minute recess to review today's discussion." She checked the clock on the wall. "When we return, we'll announce our final decision on the Hadley Cove development project."

16

Sam

Sam couldn't stop his leg from bouncing as Mayor Williams and the council members filed back in. His palm was damp against Katie's, but he held on.

The mayor stepped up to the microphone, barely glancing at the crowd. "After careful review, we've decided to move forward with the Hadley Cove development project, beginning on Main Street next week."

A collective breath sucked the air from the room.

Whispers replaced the hopeful chatter, people pulled their loved ones close, and a few let out shaky breaths that turned into tears. As the sound of crying drifted forward from the back of the room, Sam felt his chest grow heavy, watching the townspeople—who were starting to feel less like strangers—absorb the blow.

Then he spotted Derek gathering his things, along with the council members, already making a beeline for the door. Sam recognized that look on Derek's face—the same one the man wore at project meetings right before telling a family they had to sell.

A muscle in Sam's jaw twitched. After everything they had done—the speeches, the costumes, the whole town showing up—it hadn't made any difference. He glanced at Katie, who was staring straight ahead like she couldn't quite believe it was over.

Pain lanced through him at the defeat in her eyes, but his mind was already racing through alternatives. He'd spent his entire career finding solutions to impossible problems, and he wasn't about to stop now—not when it meant watching Katie lose everything she'd fought so hard to protect.

No. This wasn't over. He didn't have a plan yet—but he would. He had to. There was always an angle, always a way. For Katie, for this town, for all the people who deserved better than Derek's bottom line. If there was even the smallest chance to stop this, he would figure it out.

Sam had barely released a breath when a voice shattered the stunned silence.

"Wait!"

Sam's head snapped up. He knew that voice.

In the front row stood the old man from the Wishing Tree. He looked like he had aged ten years since last night.

What's his name again?

He still wore yesterday's button-down, now rumpled like he'd either slept in it—*if* he had slept at all.

The old man made his way to the podium. His dress shoes clacked against the steps, echoing in the dead-quiet room. He gripped the sides of the podium like he might fall over without support. "Name's Raymond Barnes. I'm the city building inspector."

Sam's mind stuttered. *The building inspector?*

The mayor's eye-roll stalled mid-motion, and Derek's smirk vanished faster than free doughnuts at a morning staff meeting.

"Life's thrown me some curveballs lately." Raymond's voice shook, but he kept going. "And I made some choices I'm not proud of. But yesterday, I met someone who reminded me that we'll never regret doing the right thing, no matter how hard it is—that we can always begin again."

A ripple of whispers skittered through the crowd. Even the teens in the back lifted their heads from their screens. Sam's heart pounded as Raymond caught his eye, and he saw the same tired face from last night—but different now, like someone who had finally decided to stop running.

"This project wasn't about helping Hadley Cove. It never was." Raymond straightened up. "Derek Huntington bribed me to falsify building inspection reports. No excuses—I messed up. All I can do now is ask for your forgiveness and do whatever it takes to fix this."

Derek jumped up so fast his chair fell over. "How dare you! You're lying!" His perfect suit couldn't hide how red his face was getting.

"Am I?" Raymond pulled out his phone, and he held it up to the microphone before hitting play.

Derek's unmistakable voice crackled through the speaker: "Look, Raymond, I heard about your grandson, Tommy, and the surgery. Tough break. But I can help—say, a hundred grand? Easy money. Just tweak those inspections the way we talked about ..."

Sam scanned the room, zeroing in on Derek, whose face had turned whiter than his starched collar.

Mrs. Waters dropped her Mary Poppins umbrella with a clatter that startled everyone.

The teenagers by the fountain stood there with their phones down, probably wishing they'd caught this on video instead.

Ada's mouth hung open without a word coming out of it—perhaps the first time in history she'd been speechless.

Ruth and George from the hardware store exchanged wide-eyed glances that mirrored the shock spreading through the room.

The recording kept going, laying out every dirty detail. How Derek had picked which buildings to target. How he'd planned to pressure people into selling. Sam's stomach turned as he recognized some of the same tactics Derek had tried using on him.

The mayor grabbed her microphone as Derek hustled out the back exit. Her voice had lost that politician's smoothness. "The Hadley Cove development project is suspended pending investigation." She then made her own exit, the council members right behind her, with Raymond disappearing through a side door after the recording came to an end.

For a second, nobody moved.

The AC kicked on with a rattle that made half the room jump.

Then—pandemonium erupted!

Old Pete hugged Ruth from the hardware store so hard his

staff knocked over a chair. Emma squatted and threw her arms around Riley as her laughter blended with his excited barks. The Martinez kids started running around in circles, forgetting their cardboard shields. Even the teens, who had been half-distracted earlier, raised their phones—probably livestreaming every second.

Before Sam could process what had happened, Katie launched herself into his arms, her legs wrapping around him like she had no intention of ever letting go. Then she kissed him, and everything else just kind of ... faded. Except for her fingers tangled in his hair, messing it up more than usual—but he couldn't care less.

When she pulled back, with a grin from ear to ear, the taste of her cherry lip balm lingered between them. He had to steady himself against a chair to keep from falling over. "What'd I do to deserve that?"

Her beautiful brown eyes gleamed. "Everything. The repairs, helping me practice, believing in me, showing up in this silly costume." She glanced at his cravat, then back to his eyes. "Why didn't you tell me?"

"Tell you what?"

"About Elizabeth. About how the store used to be yours. How you had to sell it."

His stomach dropped, and he set her down carefully, but kept her close. The celebration dimmed to white noise as memories rushed back—signing those papers, watching Elizabeth try to hide how much it hurt, knowing they had no choice. His hands tightened on Katie's waist without meaning to.

"You had enough to deal with." He swallowed hard. "And

this work trip to Hadley Cove—it started out being about me, about finding Elizabeth's wish. But then I met you at the Wishing Tree, and it became something more. It became about you. And somehow, over this weekend, it turned into us."

"Us?" She blinked like she wasn't sure she had heard him right.

"Yeah, us." His heart drummed against his ribs as the words tumbled out.

Somehow, under the fluorescent lights, she looked even more gorgeous than she had that first night at the Wishing Tree. His hand trembled as he reached for hers, afraid he'd scare her away by moving too fast.

Then the realization struck him ... He hadn't just stumbled into something with Katie; he had been falling from the moment she smiled at him under the Wishing Tree. This wasn't just an attraction. It was something deeper, something terrifying in its intensity that demanded to be felt, to be acknowledged.

And he couldn't hold it back anymore.

"I know it's crazy, and I probably sound insane. And I know it's only been a few days, but somehow, it feels like I've lived a thousand moments with you. You've made me feel alive again. And-and I didn't plan for this, but ..." He exhaled. "I love you, Katie."

She leaned into his hand, while looking into his eyes with that smile. "I love you too, Sam."

The celebration roared on around them. Apparently, Old Pete—who could have moonlighted as Gandalf—had convinced the crowd to belt out "We Are The Champions" in wildly off-key unison. Emma was at the podium doing her best Hermione impression. The Martinez kids were trying to teach Riley to bow like he was actually from Narnia, but instead he kept flopping onto his back for belly rubs.

Not that Sam noticed much of it. Right now, his whole world was just this—him and Katie, starting something that felt new yet undeniably right. And in this moment, he understood that some wishes came true in the shape of someone's smile.

He thought about Elizabeth's wish, about learning to love and be loved again. Maybe this was what she meant—allowing himself to embrace happiness in a way that let him build something different, yet just as real. Perhaps that's what second chances truly are—not a return to what was lost, but a gentle nudge toward something just as beautiful waiting to be found.

Katie squeezed his hand, and he squeezed back. Whatever came next, they'd face it together. The store still needed work—but that's what Sam did best.

And this time he would be fixing it up for them. He would make Katie's dream a reality and revive the heartbeat of Elizabeth's legacy.

Old Pete's voice boomed over the revelry. "Speech! C'mon, we need a speech from the lovebirds!"

Katie buried her face in Sam's chest, her laughter muffled against him. "No way—not another speech."

Sam pulled her closer. "Relax, I've got this." He raised his voice. "Free books for everyone!"

Katie smacked his arm. "That's NOT how business works!"

"Okay, fine—" Sam pretended to think. "Buy one, get one free?"

She shook her head but continued smiling. "You're ridiculous."

"Yeah," he said with a lopsided grin. "But you love me anyway."

"I do." She stood on her tiptoes, pressing another soft kiss against his lips. "I really do."

Epilogue

One Year Later

"And don't forget—story time moves to four o'clock next week!" Katie called out as a mom wrangled a fussy toddler into a stroller.

The place buzzed with the kind of energy she'd only dreamed about. Golden-hour rays streamed through the new skylight, warming the hardwood floors Katie had picked out herself. The air carried the scent of coffee from their new café, laced with something sweet—vanilla, maybe. Handwritten book quotes curled around the walls in Sam's script—some borrowed from Elizabeth's old journal.

Katie wound her way through the store, past Jenny ringing up the usual crowd of regulars, until she reached Elizabeth's Reading Corner. Purple throw pillows dotted the reading nook, while mason jars of fresh lavender sprigs lined the windowsill behind the cushioned bench. A vintage glass vase of deep purple irises sat beneath the brass plaque that dedicated the space. Above it all, the mural still stole her breath—woodland creatures poised as if caught mid-motion, a rabbit in glasses reading to an enchanted audience of squirrels and deer, while butterflies flitted between toadstools that sparkled with tiny painted stars.

Sam never would have asked for it, which made surprising him even sweeter. The day Katie had revealed it, she'd made him walk in blindfolded.

"Just a few more steps," she'd said, guiding him by the shoulders.

When she'd untied the bandana, he'd gone completely still, eyes scanning every detail of the mural, then said, "This is exactly how Elizabeth would have imagined it."

Of all Sam's ideas—and he had many—the Little Free Libraries had blossomed into something special. They'd started with three, then five, and now twelve of them brightened the town's corners, each bearing the Breezy Tails logo. The project had brought in so many new readers, especially kids who'd never had easy access to books before. Her favorite, shaped like a lighthouse with a working solar light that winked at passersby after dark, stood outside the elementary school.

"Miss Katie!" A little girl with untied shoelaces tugged her sleeve. "I need another dragon book. I read the last one in two days!"

"Alright, let's find you something good, princess." Katie led her to the fantasy section, where Sam's floor-to-ceiling shelves made her feel like she was in her own fairy tale. She remembered the day he had installed the rolling ladder, how he insisted on testing it himself about fifty times "just to be sure." The memory still made her smile.

"Here's one about a dragon poet who keeps setting his poems on fire by accident."

The girl clutched the book, grinning as she raced off to show her mom.

Katie watched her go, remembering those nights she had spent convincing herself she was going to lose this place. Now it thrived—Jenny at the register, Mark restocking the local authors' section that had exploded since they had started those Wednesday night writing workshops. Turns out, Hadley Cove had always been full of storytellers—just waiting for their chance.

Benny waddled over, his tags jingling. He moved a little slower now, his face dusted with more gray, but his eyes still held that familiar spark. His orthopedic beds had multiplied—one near the kids' books, another tucked by the mysteries, and his favorite, right by the window, where he could watch the world go by. The vet said he was doing great for his age. Katie figured the steady stream of belly rubs and treats from customers had something to do with it.

The storage room door creaked open and Sam appeared, wiping dust off those jeans she kept trying to replace. Managing the Historic District renovation kept him busy these days—a project that had grown so successful he'd finally paid off the last of his debt three months ago, though he'd tried to downplay that milestone. He still showed up a few times a week to Breezy Tails, usually with peach cobbler muffins and a brand-new idea she'd pretend was ridiculous before secretly falling in love with it. Just yesterday, he had suggested turning the old gazebo into a reading nook for summer evenings.

"Ready to go?" He walked over to her and brushed a kiss against her cheek. "Don't want to be late."

"Almost." Katie gathered her things, doing one last scan of the store.

The Halloween display needs work—maybe something with ravens? And that author event next week—

The bell chimed. Katie barely had time to brace herself before Ada swept in on a cloud of flowery perfume. "Well, well, well! If it ain't my favorite lovebirds!"

Benny's tail went crazy as Ada bent to scratch his ears.

"We actually need to—" Katie tried.

But Ada plowed ahead. "Did you hear about Derek? It was all over The Facebook. Five years in the can! And that fine—hundred thousand dollars!" She yanked a church bulletin from her massive purse to fan herself. "Would take me ten lifetimes to pay that on my social security check. Not that anyone's counting, mind you."

Sam squeezed Katie's hand, fighting back a laugh.

"And Raymond Barnes?" Ada pushed her blue glasses up her nose. "Lost his license, but no fine, thank goodness with Tommy's medical bills and all. That boy's doing so much better since the surgery. Saw him at the park yesterday, moving like nothing ever happened. His grandfather might have made some mistakes, but love makes people do crazy things sometimes, doesn't it?"

"Ada, we really need to—"

"Oh my, look at the time!" She glanced at her empty

wrist. "I'm late for my ... thing." She bustled out, leaving them in a trail of perfume.

Katie and Sam broke into laughter. Even Benny let out a confused bark.

"That's our Ada," Sam said, holding the door while Katie clipped on Benny's leash.

Walking to the Wishing Tree, Katie's mind wandered back to that first night—how close she had come to giving up, how one chance encounter had changed everything. The town felt different now. Storefronts gleamed with fresh paint, and flowers spilled from window boxes. But the soul of the place remained, maybe even stronger than before.

Nearing the Wishing Tree, she stopped short at the sight before her.

A crowd had gathered under the tree—Martinez kids still sporting streaks of festival face paint, Old Pete steadying himself on his cane, Ruth and George from the hardware store hand-in-hand, and Emma barely keeping Riley from bounding into the chaos. Phil from the diner stood with them, beaming in his *Best Breakfast in Town* apron, having clearly rushed over straight from the kitchen. They formed a half-circle, all wearing looks that made Katie's stomach flip.

The sunset painted everything in shades of gold and pink, which glinted off ribbons dancing in the breeze. Wildflowers dotted the ground—the old wishes that had somehow taken root and bloomed into something real.

Sam took her hand, guiding her to the very spot where it had all begun.

"Katie." His voice was soft but steady, the way it always

was when he meant every word. "You taught me that beginning again isn't about erasing the past. It's about honoring what was, while giving yourself room to grow into what's next." His thumb brushed over her knuckles. "You gave me that space, and now—"

He dropped to one knee.

Katie's hand flew to her mouth.

"I love you. Will you marry me?"

"Yes!" She barely let him finish. "Yes, yes, yes!"

The crowd erupted as Sam slipped the ring on her finger. Katie threw her arms around him, kissing him while Benny barked his approval. Old Pete pulled out his handkerchief, dabbing at his eyes while trying to hide behind it. The Martinez kids pulled crumpled flower petals from their pockets and sent them fluttering into the air. Emma cried into Riley's fur and someone shouted something about wedding planning that Katie chose to ignore for now.

"Wait." She pulled back, heart racing. "I want to show you something."

She led him to a faded blue ribbon tied low on a branch. Despite sun and rain, the words were still clear:

Please help me save my store.

Katie

"Guess wishes do come true." She smiled up at him, knowing how this place had saved her in ways she'd never expected.

"They sure do." He kissed her temple.

They stood where Sam had once searched for Elizabeth's wish, where Katie had almost given up, where everything had somehow begun. Benny flopped at their feet with a contented groan that seemed to say *finally*.

"Let's make a new one? Together?" Sam asked.

Katie nodded. "I'll write it. We both know your handwriting is a crime against humanity."

Sam scoffed, pulling a yellow ribbon and tag from the stand. "Fair enough. Though you seem to read my coffee maker sticky notes just fine."

"That's because I've had practice decoding your love letters." She grinned, taking the pen he offered. "I do love how you draw little hearts over the 'i' in my name."

Sam smiled, and in that moment, surrounded by their friends and the community who had become family, Katie thought that maybe this was the real magic of the Wishing Tree—not that it granted wishes exactly, but the way it gave people the courage to reach for them and recognize when they had already come true.

She leaned in, whispered their wish in Sam's ear, and watched as his face softened into something unshakably sure.

Then wrote:

May everyone have more stories,
more love, and more chances to begin again—together.
Katie and Sam.

He stretched to tie it up high among the others while everyone cheered.

With Sam's arm looped around her waist and Benny pressed against her leg, she realized that the best wishes weren't the ones you made, but the ones life led you to when you were finally ready to see them.

I hope you enjoyed the story, but your stay in Hadley Cove doesn't have to end today ...

Read Wendi's story next!

Wendi Parker didn't believe in love until she came back to Hadley Cove.

Wendi Parker thought she'd left her small-town life for good when she moved to New York City. But after a failed marriage and a career that's going nowhere, she's back in Hadley Cove, accompanied by her rescue dog, Max.

Miles Harrison, a retired army captain, has also returned to Hadley Cove to heal and to look after his aging father. When Max unexpectedly dashes off and leads Wendi to Miles, the chemistry between them is undeniable. As they spend time together, the town's Fourth of July celebration isn't the only thing lighting up.

Will they overcome the scars of their pasts and plan a future together? Or will the town that brought them together also tear them apart?

Get your signed copy at kerkmurray.com.

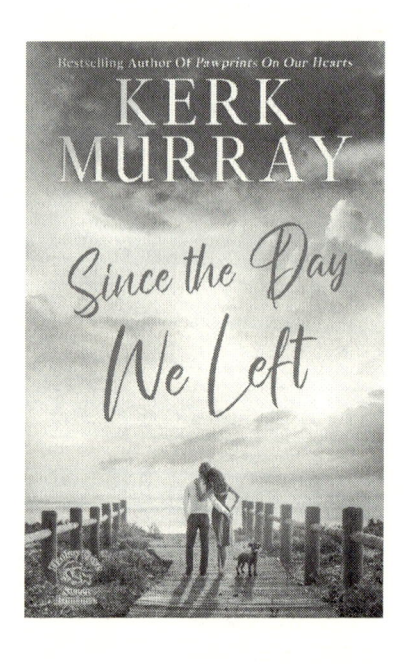

Love this book? Don't forget to leave a review!

Help others discover the *Hadley Cove Sweet Romance* series. Every review matters and it matters a lot. It can be as short as one phrase to a few sentences. Wherever you bought this book, you can use this link to leave an honest review on Amazon, Goodreads, Bookbub, or your favorite retailer:

kerkmurray.com/products/reviewsincethedaywewished

Get signed paperbacks up to 40% Off

Bundle & Save at kerkmurray.com.

Apply this coupon at checkout for an additional 10% off: **GET10**

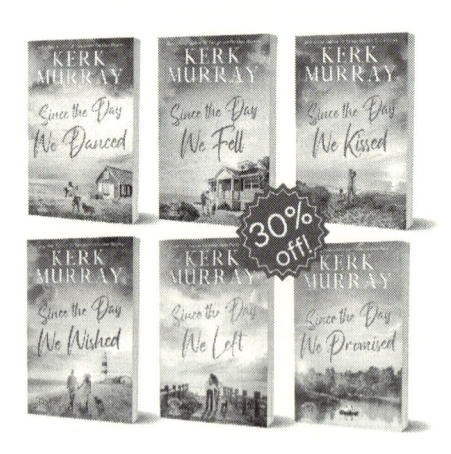

Hadley Cove Recipes

All recipes are vegan-friendly

Lisa's Peach Cobbler Muffins

To awaken the soul

Ingredients:

- 2 cups all-purpose flour
- 2/3 cup granulated sugar
- 2 teaspoons baking powder
- 1/2 teaspoon baking soda
- 1/4 teaspoon salt
- 1 teaspoon ground cinnamon

- 1/4 teaspoon ground nutmeg

- 2/3 cup plant-based milk (almond or oat)

- 1/3 cup vegetable oil

- 1/4 cup applesauce

- 2 teaspoons vanilla extract

- 2 cups fresh peaches, diced (or thawed frozen peaches)

Streusel Topping:
- 1/2 cup brown sugar

- 1/3 cup all-purpose flour

- 2 tablespoons vegan butter, melted

- 1/2 teaspoon ground cinnamon

Directions:
1. Preheat oven to 375°F (190°C). Line a 12-cup muffin tin with paper liners.

2. In a large bowl, whisk together flour, sugar, baking powder, baking soda, salt, cinnamon, and nutmeg.

3. In a separate bowl, combine plant milk, oil, applesauce, and vanilla extract.

4. Pour wet ingredients into dry ingredients, stirring just until combined. Do not overmix.

5. Gently fold in the diced peaches.

6. Fill muffin cups 2/3 full with batter.

7. For topping, combine brown sugar, flour, melted vegan butter, and cinnamon in a small bowl.

8. Sprinkle topping evenly over each muffin.

9. Bake for 20-22 minutes, or until a toothpick inserted comes out clean.

10. Cool in pan for 5 minutes before transferring to a wire rack.

11. Best served warm.

Katie's Fried Pickles

To connect with others

Ingredients:
- 1 jar dill pickle chips, drained and patted very dry
- 1 cup all-purpose flour
- 1 tablespoon cornstarch

- 1 teaspoon garlic powder

- 1 teaspoon onion powder

- 1/2 teaspoon paprika

- 1/2 teaspoon black pepper

- 1 teaspoon salt

- 3/4 cup plant-based milk (unsweetened)

- 2 tablespoons apple cider vinegar

- 1 tablespoon neutral oil

- 1 cup crushed waffle cone pieces (vegan variety)

- 1/2 cup panko breadcrumbs

Optional Toppings:
- Vegan ranch dressing

- Fresh dill for garnish

- Hot sauce

Directions:
1. Drain pickles and place between paper towels, pressing gently to remove excess moisture. Let sit for 15 minutes.

2. Combine plant milk with apple cider vinegar and let sit for 5 minutes to create a thickened milk mixture.

3. In a bowl, whisk together flour, cornstarch, garlic powder, onion powder, paprika, pepper, and salt.

4. Stir the oil into the thickened milk mixture.

5. In a food processor, pulse waffle cone pieces until they're fine crumbs. Mix with panko breadcrumbs.

6. Create a dredging station: bowl of seasoned flour, bowl of wet mixture, and bowl of waffle-panko mixture.

7. Dip each pickle first in flour, then wet mixture, then coat thoroughly with waffle-panko mixture.

8. Spray air fryer basket with oil spray. Place pickles in a single layer, not touching.

9. Spray tops of breaded pickles with oil spray.

10. Air fry at 375°F for 8-10 minutes, flipping halfway through, until golden brown and crispy.

11. Serve hot and crispy.

Phil's Lemon Poppy Seed Pancakes

To reminisce on fond memories

Ingredients:

- 1½ cups all-purpose flour
- 2 tablespoons poppy seeds
- 2 teaspoons baking powder
- 1/4 teaspoon salt
- 1/2 teaspoon baking soda
- 1/4 teaspoon salt
- 2 tablespoons granulated sugar
- 1¼ cups plant-based milk (oat or almond)
- 1/4 cup fresh lemon juice
- 2 tablespoons lemon zest
- 1/4 cup neutral oil (like canola or melted coconut oil)
- 1 teaspoon vanilla extract
- 1 tablespoon apple cider vinegar

Blueberry Syrup:
- 2 cups fresh or frozen blueberries
- 1/3 cup maple syrup
- 1 tablespoon lemon juice
- 1 tablespoon water
- 1/4 teaspoon vanilla extract

Directions:
1. In a large bowl, whisk together flour, poppy seeds, baking powder, baking soda, salt, and sugar.

2. In a separate bowl, combine plant milk, lemon juice, lemon zest, oil, vanilla extract, and apple cider vinegar. Let sit for 5 minutes.

3. Pour the wet ingredients into the dry ingredients and whisk until just combined. Some small lumps are okay - do not overmix.

4. Let batter rest for 10 minutes while you prepare the blueberry syrup.

5. For the syrup: Combine blueberries, maple syrup, lemon juice, and water in a small saucepan. Bring to a simmer over medium heat. Cook for 5-7 minutes until berries break down and sauce thickens

slightly. Remove from heat, stir in vanilla extract.

6. Heat a non-stick griddle or pan over medium heat. Lightly grease with oil.

7. Pour about 1/4 cup batter for each pancake. Cook until bubbles form on the surface (2-3 minutes).

8. Flip and cook other side until golden brown (1-2 minutes).

9. Serve warm, topped with warm blueberry syrup.

<u>Riley's Recipe Sweet Potato Chews</u>

To bribe your fur babies

Please consult with your veterinarian before making any changes to your pet's diet or feeding routine

Ingredients:
- 2 medium sweet potatoes
- 2 ripe bananas
- 20 baby carrots (approximately one 16 oz bag)
- 1/2 cup rolled oats

- 1 tablespoon coconut oil (optional)

Directions:
1. Preheat oven to 350°F (175°C).

2. Wash and dry sweet potatoes and baby carrots thoroughly.

3. Place baby carrots in a food processor and pulse until finely shredded. If you don't have a food processor, you can grate them by hand.

4. Peel and mash the bananas in a large mixing bowl.

5. Using a food processor or grater, grate the sweet potatoes.

6. Mix the shredded baby carrots, mashed bananas, and grated sweet potatoes together until well combined.

7. If using coconut oil, mix it in at this stage.

8. Line baking sheets with parchment paper.

9. Spread mixture approximately 1/4 inch thick onto the parchment paper. You can either: Make small circles (about 2 inches in diameter), spread in one large sheet to cut after baking, or use a dog bone-shaped cookie cutters to form shapes before baking.

10. Bake for 25-30 minutes, or until edges are lightly browned and center is firm.

11. Check at 20 minutes - if treats feel too moist, continue baking but check every 5 minutes to prevent burning.

12. Let cool completely on the baking sheet. They will continue to firm up as they cool.

13. Storage: Refrigerate up to 1 week or freeze up to 2 months in airtight container.

Book Club Questions

If you'd like Kerk to attend your in-person or virtual book club, please contact info@kerkmurray.com.

1. The novel opens with Katie struggling to keep her bookstore afloat. How does her relationship with the store reflect her personal journey throughout the story?

2. Sam carries deep grief over losing Elizabeth and their dream of owning the bookstore. How does his past influence his initial interactions with Katie?

3. Discuss the symbolism of the Wishing Tree. How does it serve as both a physical and metaphorical connection point throughout the story?

4. How do Katie's experiences with Derek impact her ability to trust and form new relationships? What moments show her growth in overcoming these past hurts?

5. The novel features many supporting characters from the town. Which secondary character did you find most memorable and why?

6. Compare and contrast how Sam and Katie each handle their respective losses—Sam's loss of Elizabeth and Katie's loss of her marriage and self-confidence.

7. The bookstore serves as more than just a setting. How does it function as a character in its own right?

8. Discuss the role of community in the novel. How does the town come together during the climactic town hall scene?

9. What do you think about the pacing of Sam and Katie's relationship? Did their quick connection feel authentic given their circumstances?

10. How does Benny's character contribute to both the plot and character development? What role does he play in bringing Sam and Katie together?

11. The author uses flashbacks to reveal important background information. How effective were these in helping you understand the characters?

12. Discuss the theme of second chances throughout the novel. How do different characters experience and embrace new beginnings?

13. What role does Ada play in the story? How does her gossip both help and hinder the main characters?

14. Compare Elizabeth's final wish with what actually unfolds in the story. How does this affect your interpretation of the novel's events?

15. How does the author use the bookstore's possible closure to explore themes of change versus preservation in small towns?

16. Discuss the significance of Derek's appearance at the town hall meeting. How does this confrontation allow Katie to show her growth?

17. What do you think about Raymond Barnes's character arc and redemption? Was his confession satisfying?

18. How does the author use various literary references and book-related events to enhance the story?

19. Discuss the symbolism of the wildflowers growing from old wishes. What does this suggest about the relationship between dreams and reality?

20. How does Emma's friendship support Katie's character development throughout the story?

21. Compare the different types of love portrayed in the novel—romantic, friendship, community, etc. How do they interact and influence each other?

22. Discuss the significance of Sam's choice to turn down Derek's offer. What does this reveal about his character?

23. How does the author use the setting of Hadley Cove to enhance the themes of the story?

24. What role does *Pride and Prejudice* play in the story?

25. Discuss the significance of the epilogue. How does it provide closure while honoring both the past and future?

26. How does the author handle the delicate balance of honoring Elizabeth's memory while allowing Sam to find new love?

27. What does the novel suggest about the importance of small businesses in maintaining a town's identity?

28. How do both main characters overcome their fears throughout the story? What catalyzes these changes?

29. Discuss the various ways books and storytelling serve as connecting points between characters in the novel.

30. The novel explores the tension between progress and preservation. How do different characters define and value "progress" differently, and what

does the story ultimately suggest about balancing change with tradition?

Giving Back

"Never underestimate the power of a small group of committed people to change the world. In fact, it is the only thing that ever has."

—Margaret Mead

"Together redeeming the lives of animals and ending their suffering through our compassion."

THE LEXI'S LEGACY
FOUNDATION INC

Kerk Murray's readers make a difference. Since the release of his memoir, *Pawprints On Our Hearts*, his generous readers have raised over $20,000 toward the care of abused animals through book proceeds as well as donations to the nonprofit he founded, *The Lexi's Legacy Foundation*. If you feel compelled to donate, you can do so right here:

donorbox.org/everydollarmatters

Here's a list of the animal rescue organizations that readers are supporting monthly through each Kerk Murray book sale:

1. 2nd Street Hooligans Rescue – California
2. Cuddly – California
3. Little Hill Sanctuary – California
4. Love Always Sanctuary – California
5. Sale Ranch Animal Sanctuary – California
6. The Shore Sanctuary – California
7. Viva Global Rescue – California
8. Road To Refuge Animal Sanctuary – Connecticut
9. The Riley Farm Sanctuary – Connecticut
10. Love Life Animal Rescue & Sanctuary – Florida
11. Live Freely Sanctuary – Florida
12. Operation Liberation – Florida
13. SAGE Sanctuary and Gardens for Education – Florida
14. Farm of the Free – Georgia
15. Humane Society Greater Savannah – Georgia
16. Society of Humane Friends of Georgia – Georgia
17. Ruby Slipper Goat Rescue – Kansas

18. Shy 38 Inc. – Kansas

19. Sowa Goat Sanctuary – Massachusetts

20. Angela's Ark – North Carolina

21. Billie's Buddies Animal Rescue – North Carolina

22. Fairytale Farm Animal Sanctuary – North Carolina

23. Blackbird Animal Refuge – New Jersey

24. Broncs and Buns Rescue and Rehab – New Jersey

25. Fawn's Fortress – New Jersey

26. Happily Ever After Farm – New Jersey

27. Goats of Anarchy – New Jersey

28. Maddie & Sven's Rescue Sanctuary – New Jersey

29. Marley Meadows Animal Sanctuary – New Jersey

30. Old Fogey Farm – New Jersey

31. Rancho Relaxo – New Jersey

32. Runaway Farm – New Jersey

33. Troll House Animal Sanctuary – New Jersey

34. Wild Lands Wild Horse Fund – New Jersey

35. Happy Compromise Farm – New York

36. Sleepy Pig Farm Animal Sanctuary – New York

37. Woodstock Farm Sanctuary – New York

38. Enchanted Farm Sanctuary – Oregon

39. Harmony Farm Sanctuary – Oregon

40. Morningside Farm Sanctuary – Oregon

41. Charlie's Army Animal Rescue – Pennsylvania

42. Happy Heart Happy Home Farm & Rescue – Pennsylvania

43. The Philly Kitty Club – Pennsylvania

44. The Misfit Farm – Texas

45. Best Friends Animal Society – Utah

46. Harmony Farm Sanctuary and Wellness Center – Vermont

47. Off The Plate Farm Animal Sanctuary – Vermont

48. Gentle Acres Animal Haven – Virginia

49. Little Buckets Farm Sanctuary – Virginia

About the Author

Kerk Murray is the international bestselling and award-winning author of *Pawprints On Our Hearts* and the *Hadley Cove Sweet Romance* series. He's a romantic at heart, with a passion for celebrating life, love, and the beautiful connections between humans and animals. His soulful stories capture the essence of opening oneself up to the possibilities that love can bring, and the magic that can unfold when we do.

If you're a fan of sweet, clean and wholesome, swoon-worthy romance stories that will leave you feeling uplifted and inspired, then his novels are a must-read.

Kerk is also the founder of *The Lexi's Legacy Foundation*, a coastal Georgia 501(c)(3) nonprofit organization committed to ending animal suffering. A portion of his books' proceeds are donated to the nonprofit and together with the support of his readers, the lives of hundreds of abused animals have been changed forever.

Join him on his mission in creating a more compassionate world for all living beings, one heartwarming story at a time.

Follow Kerk on social media and sign up for his mailing list at **kerkmurray.com** to stay updated on his latest releases and sneak peeks into his upcoming works.

amazon.com/stores/Kerk-Murray/author/B09C39NLYT

goodreads.com/author/show/21719388.Kerk_Murray

bookbub.com/profile/kerk-murray

instagram.com/kerkmurray

facebook.com/kerkwrites

tiktok.com/@kerkmurray

Made in the USA
Columbia, SC
09 February 2025